ALPHA MALE

ALPHA MALE

MIKE WALSH

To order additional copies of this book, contact:
Xlibris Corporation
1-888-795-4274
www.Xlibris.com
Orders@Xlibris.com
14935

This book is dedicated to Terri who was always there.

THE EARLY 1990s

CHAPTER 1

The wolves were restless.

A storm was coming. At dusk it snowed gently, the large flakes drifting down from a windless sky. Lucy watched from the kitchen window of the cabin. She was almost seventy miles north of Fairbanks, a stone's throw by Alaska standards. The cabin was situated in a flat glen surrounded by dense woods. She could see the portion of the log lean-to where the wolves always gathered in bad weather. Her husband, Miles Coffin, had erected it just inside the perimeter of the wire fence enclosure that contained six fully grown timber wolves. The shelter was about one hundred yards from the cabin. As inadequate as it appeared, it served its purpose well.

The wolves had already gathered inside the shelter even though the storm had hardly begun. It could be a bad one, Lucy thought; the wolves already knew. As the wind came with the bleak night the freezing rain settled heavily in layers of ice on the pines, bending and straining the limbs. Lucy began to worry. She had seen ice storms before. A fallen tree could do great damage especially if it hit the garage where the generator was housed. Miles Coffin had taken the precaution to make sure power was continuous during the long winter months. Without electricity they could not exist. The nearest neighbor was more than three miles away. The luxury of electric power had not yet reached their isolated world.

Coffin had gone south to Fairbanks and wouldn't return for at least another twenty-four hours. He was considered somewhat of an authority on wolves and had been hired for his valued input by the producers of a conservationist film about the mistreatment of wildlife, wolves in particular. Lucy and Miles Coffin raised a wolf pack in captivity and studied their habits and social order.

The way the storm was building she wasn't sure she'd see Coffin for a much longer time. The roads would be slick with ice by morning and would be almost impossible to travel. She worried more about his safety than her own predicament.

She had been through lonely periods in adverse conditions before. Coffin was continually away on conservationist film trips, as a guide for hunting parties or hired by the Game and Fish Department to oversee the quota of wolves killed. It was the routine their lives had taken; he away and she at home. She had learned early in their relationship to cope with the long waits. There was plenty of food, water, and fuel to take her through the most difficult times. Once, she had been snowbound for weeks and had survived without any life-threatening incidents. She had cut a path through a foot of snow and brought food to the wolves, who, because they were penned in, depended totally on her. When Coffin showed up he was amazed that this small woman had accomplished so much in the face of adversity.

Lucy was startled by a loud crackling noise and a crash above the steady sound of the freezing rain. She saw where a large branch had come down across the driveway not more than sixty feet from the house. The jeep was parked in the garage which Coffin had the resourcefulness to heat; a dead battery could be as bad as the loss of power in the house.

She would have a difficult time getting the jeep past the limb to the road if she had to leave. The driveway was completely blocked. Coffin would also have trouble getting in.

She glanced at the fenced pen where the wolf pack hovered in the shelter. A large, old pine came crashing to the ground, broken off at the base, unable to bear the enormous weight of the frozen rain that clung to it. As it struck the frozen earth thousands of crystals of cracked ice flew through the air. The top of the old tree landed directly on the shelter where the wolves had gathered. Through the noise she heard howls of pain and terror.

She watched to see if any wolves had been injured. Only three emerged from the crushed lean-to. She threw on a heavy jacket, slipped on her boots and grabbed a flashlight. She went out into the frightful night directly to the garage and climbed the stairs to the second-floor loft. She and Coffin had built an observation area in a corner with ample windows providing a view of the penned compound where the wolves were kept. Set on a tripod was a video camera aimed at the lean-to and the area surrounding it.

Lucy could see the wolves moving in the pen but could not yet determine if any had been injured by the fallen tree. She would have to go into the area and check the animals personally. Out of habit, she clicked on the camera and let it run. Whatever the problem with the wolves, she would have it documented on tape.

She went back outside and headed for the penned area, slipping a few times as she crossed the distance to the gate that locked the wolves inside the enclosure. The rain was freezing as it landed, the entire surface of the ground now one continuous sheet of ice. She walked through a glistening wonderland, wondering what Coffin was doing at that precise moment. Was he on his way home? She knew he must be worried. He was a hundred or so miles away and certainly feeling the effects of the storm.

She shivered as icy water trickled down her neck, tightened the hood of her jacket, and braced herself for the task ahead. If one or more of the wolves were injured she would have to care for them. The animals were jittery from the storm, and the sudden shock of a tree crashing into their shelter must have totally unnerved them.

Ice was already encrusting the latch that held the gate to the pen locked in place. Lucy chipped at it with the butt of the flash-light until she was able to unlock it. She swung the gate open slowly, stepped inside the enclosure and let the latch fall into place behind her. She didn't want any of the wolves getting out in the brutal night. It would be impossible trying to locate a missing wolf in the storm.

The beam of light from the flashlight cut raggedly through the falling rain. She crossed the enclosure to where the pine had fallen against the lean-to. Some of the logs from the walls and roof had been caved in and the entrance was blocked by branches of the huge, dead tree.

She couldn't see any wolves from her position.

She moved closer to the shelter until she was at the entrance and swung the beam of light into the opening, letting it drift around the interior of the small space. Odd, she thought. She couldn't find any wolves inside. It seemed that at least one of them might have been hurt. Where had they all gone?

She turned, her ears picking up the sound of movement be-hind her. Aiming the flashlight at the source of the sound, Lucy saw Midnight, a large black wolf, the acknowledged leader of the pack. The huge animal was crouched on the icy surface, not ten feet from Lucy, his black lips curled in a vicious snarl as he growled.

"Midnight," Lucy called. "What's wrong?"

The flashlight beam picked up other wolves behind the black male. Rigidly in position, they watched and waited. Midnight barked suddenly and, lifting his head toward the sky, he began to howl. The other wolves joined in, crying out at the storm, their shrill wails sending shivers through her body.

"Midnight," Lucy shouted, her voice quivering. "Stop!" She tried to sound firm but she knew she wasn't.

The wolf turned and faced her squarely, the light falling full on his face. His eyes glowed brightly, turning liquid green. He snarled again at Lucy and crouched, threatening, ready to spring.

If only she had thought to bring with her the .45 automatic Coffin had left for emergencies.

The wolf sprang.

Oh, God! No!

He landed flush on Lucy, knocking the flashlight from her hand and driving her to the hard, cold ground. The wolf quickly mounted her body and ripped at her throat in one swift motion. The other wolves, behind him, became frenzied and charged the fallen human, tearing at her vulnerable flesh with savage ferocity.

Lucy's last thoughts were of Miles Coffin and how senseless it was for him to worry now.

CHAPTER 2

M iles Coffin found the trapped wolf a mile ahead of the three-man party he was leading to locate hurt or starving animals thirty miles east of Fairbanks. Many forest creatures had been wounded by gunshots or maimed by traps and left to suffer and starve because they could not hunt for food.

The wolf was a gray female. The steel trap had slammed shut on her right forepaw. Trying to free herself from the pain, she had pulled the heavy metal instrument across the snow, but the drag hook that was attached to six feet of steel chain worked like an anchor. It kept her hobbled and tired her quickly.

The wolf watched Coffin approach. She began to howl, a tortured, piteous cry. She was pleading for assistance to end her pain and confusion. Over the years Coffin had often witnessed scenes like this when he had been a wolf hunter. Many snared wolves chewed away the crushed paw, releasing themselves only to face a slower death, crippled and unable to hunt.

The wolf had stretched the chain, holding her paw off the ground and trying desperately to pull free. To Coffin it seemed as if she had lifted the injured paw to show him her injury.

The three members of the expedition were about a quarter

mile behind him, slowed by the cameras and photo equipment they carried. Coffin figured it would be at least ten minutes before they caught up to him. He wanted to free the animal immediately and end its terror, but he knew the conservationists wanted to get this incident recorded for their project.

As Coffin got closer the hurt animal drew back its black lips in a snarl revealing a set of worn fangs. She was older than he thought.

"Don't be afraid, old girl," Coffin said, keeping his voice soft. "I won't hurt you."

Coffin approached cautiously, keeping his attention on the wolf. She was not large, weighing, he guessed, about seventy-five pounds. But he was aware of the power in her jaws that could snap his wrist or tear out his throat.

The trap was an old Newhouse no. 14. He hadn't seen one of those in a while. It had taken a deep bite into flesh and bone. The wolf had stepped into the trap squarely and it gripped her at the joint of her paw. The wicked steel had torn through ligaments and had held fast. Even if the wolf had escaped she would have a useless paw and would limp the rest of her life.

"A few more minutes and we'll get you out," he said.

He ran back to the edge of the ravine. The men were only a few hundred yards from him on the snowy slope.

"Come on," he shouted. "Snap it up. I found something I think you'd want on film."

When the men got to the trapped animal they quickly set up their equipment.

"My God, Coffin," the leader of the group said. "Why do men do this?"

"Something I've never been able to figure out," Coffin replied.

"Can we get him out of there?

"Her," Coffin said. "She's a female. Yes. We'll use a muzzle."

"Let me set up the cameras before you start," the man said. "I want to get some tight shots. Then we'll get you releasing the wolf. There's no danger. Is there?"

"To you or the wolf?" Coffin asked.

The conservationist didn't answer.

"Just be careful," Coffin said. "She can hurt you badly if she feels threatened."

The men had their cameras ready. They were taking shots of the wounded wolf from different angles. Coffin assembled a noose on a pole and moved closer to the gray wolf.

"Easy, old girl," he said gently. "I'll have you out in a minute."

After two tries he looped the muzzle around her neck. He tightened it and handed the pole to the man who had spoken to him.

"Hold her tight," he said while the wolf kicked. "Don't choke her."

He dropped another loop around the wolf's head and led it in the opposite direction. He handed this line to another of the crew. The man took the line and held fast.

"Now hold her steady for a minute," Coffin ordered.

The old wolf was pulling fiercely against the strain of the lines around her neck and against the grip of the trap. Coffin used one hand and his right foot to open the jagged steel teeth. The wolf pulled her damaged paw free. She sprang back quickly and the lines pulled taut.

Coffin stepped over her back and mounted her. He drew his hunting knife from its sheath and sliced the binds. He stepped away from the wolf. She turned and stumbled off over the field of snow and disappeared in a wooded knoll.

"Great stuff," the cameraman shouted. "I got it all."

"Will there ever be an end to this kind of brutality?" The leader of the group said to Coffin. "Can we ever stop it?"

"I doubt it," Coffin answered.

* * *

The snow turned to rain and then to ice. Before Coffin got outside the limits of Fairbanks he had skidded twice on the road, turning almost a complete circle both times. He fretted about

Lucy—alone in a storm and no one to help her with the wolf pack. He became worried when he telephoned her, the phone ringing over a dozen times with no answer.

If the roads were badly iced north of Fairbanks he might not get home at all tonight. He planned to drive there as soon as he finished his commitment to the film producers. When he saw how bad the weather was getting he decided to leave immediately. He traveled slowly, keeping to the center of the road. Ice formed on the windshield but turned to slush from the interior warmth of the Range Rover. He was able to see while the wipers didn't freeze.

He felt he shouldn't have tried returning home until the storm ended but he sensed something was wrong that Lucy didn't respond to the ringing phone. He hoped the storm didn't trap him completely along the way. If he got iced down he wouldn't make it before morning. As he drove slower now, more cautiously, he looked for some kind of shelter. Just in case.

How bad was the storm at home, he wondered. Were the phone lines down? Was Lucy all right? If she was injured, was she able to remain calm? He had great faith in her, but he didn't want her worrying about him. If the ice was collecting heavily on the trees surrounding the house Lucy could be in for some trouble. The wolves would huddle in the lean-to. Lucy would be concerned for their safety and might attempt to calm their fears. They were bound to be jittery. Perhaps, he thought, that was why she didn't respond to the ringing phone. She was with the wolves at the pen when he called.

Coffin was about to give up and pull off the road when the freezing rain let up a little. He drove the next twenty miles relatively unchallenged, picking up speed, before he hit heavier rain again. But it was a bit warmer now and the rain was not freezing so quickly. The storm was right over him.

By the time he finally pulled onto his property the ice on the main roads was slushy. The storm was passing over rapidly. When he turned into the drive he saw the large limb that was blocking his way. He stopped the Range Rover and walked around the debris toward the house. The lights were on. He prayed Lucy was inside, safe. By his watch it was nearly two a.m. She might be sleeping. She wouldn't have expected him until morning. Then the lights should have been turned off. As he got nearer he saw that a fallen tree had landed on the lean-to inside the fenced enclosure.

There must have been trouble with the wolves. Lucy might be in danger right now. He was glad he had pushed himself to get here tonight.

He moved faster and crossed the distance to the house in a few running leaps. He threw the door open and stepped inside.

"Lucy!" he called, his voice nervous and cracking.

No answer. He repeated his cry. Still no reply. She must be out in the pen, he thought. One of the wolves might have been hurt when the tree came down. Hurry.

He ran across the ice towards the fenced pen.

"Lucy!" he cried out. "Where are you?"

As he ran unsteadily he saw a dim light near the ground shining through the dense branches of the fallen tree. It was not moving. What was it?

As he got to the gate he realized the cone-shaped wedge of light he saw was a flashlight lying on the snow. Coffin gasped under his breath. Could the tree have fallen on Lucy while she was in the lean-to tending to one of the wolves?

He lifted the latch and stepped inside the fenced area, getting quickly to the spot. He picked up the flashlight and sprayed the light around the area inside the shelter.

Lucy was nowhere to be seen.

"Lucy!" he screamed, desperation in his voice. "Oh God, Lucy, where are you?"

Then he spotted the blood on the ice. She *was* hurt! Perhaps she had tried to make it back to the house and was unconscious somewhere out there on the ice.

And where were the wolves?

"Midnight! Rusty! Dawn!" he called their names.

They also did not respond.

He let the light linger on the bloodstains. It might not be Lucy's blood, he thought. One of the wolves.

He shined the light along the trail of blood. A long, thin smear of blood was easy to follow. The flashlight led the way in front of him past the fallen tree and into the edge of the woods behind the lean-to.

Not fifty feet inside the frozen clump of birch, he found the wolves crouched in a group around the partially eaten body of his wife.

Fear hit him like a burst of cold air.

"Lucy!!" he screamed. He ran to her body and knelt beside her. The wolves backed off, recognizing him.

She was dead, mutilated beyond recognition.

He screamed loudly, his painful cry like the howling of the wolves who had done this terrible thing.

He knew immediately what had happened. The wolves were spooked by the storm and the crashing tree had completely un-nerved them. Lucy must have come into the enclosure to see if any had been hurt and they attacked her. They got caught up in the frenzy of the blood lust and it had run its course.

He scooped her up and carried her to the house. He lay her on the bed and cleaned the blood from her body, sat beside her and cried some more. He found his .45 automatic in the bedroom and cocked it, slamming a round into the chamber. He stuffed a few ammunition clips in his pocket and ran back to the enclosure, the pistol held out straight in front of him.

By now, he had completely lost control. He thought only of revenge for the death of his beloved Lucy.

The flashlight held in his left hand, pistol in his right, he walked directly to where the wolves had dragged Lucy's body. They had not moved from where he had left them. He threw the light on them. The green and yellow eyes gleamed. Their ears stood straight out from their heads. There were obvious traces of Lucy's blood staining the muzzles of some.

Coffin went wild. He fired once. Twice. Blood and fur splattered across the white surface of the ground as one wolf fell. He fired again and again. Another died. And another. One wolf ran into the trees trying to hide. Another, apparently injured, just sat on the snow and watched. Coffin aimed calmly at the animal's head, pulled the trigger and blew the skull to fragments.

He charged into the trees after the one who had escaped.

"Rusty," he called out to the wolf. "Come to me, Rusty. Come and die."

It didn't take long to catch the animal. Raised in captivity, unaccustomed to danger, the wolf responded to the voice of the man he trusted, the man who fed him and took care of him. No more than a hundred feet into the thick trees that shone now like glass columns, Coffin saw the wolf coming to him.

"That's it," he implored the wolf, shining the light on him. "Come on."

The wolf sat on his haunches, waiting for him, Lucy's smeared blood on his lips. Coffin raised the .45 and shot him dead.

When he got to the fence he saw the black wolf, Midnight, waiting outside for him. Coffin had forgotten him in the frenzy of his killing spree. The wolf was prowling back and forth, pacing in a small circle. He sensed the carnage that had taken place and felt the immediate danger to himself. But he waited for his master.

Midnight had caused Lucy's death, Coffin thought. This wolf had been responsible for the uneasiness in the pack and had probably upset them during the storm. He realized Midnight would have been the one to lead the attack on Lucy. The other wolves would easily have followed him.

Coffin raised the gun and fired at him. The slug missed and chipped the ice in front of the animal. The wolf yelped and ran off into the night. He was gone quickly while Coffin fired an empty gun. How, he wondered, did the wolf get outside the fenced area? Hadn't he closed it behind him?

CHAPTER 3

Midnight trudged through the deep snow, his large paws following in the ruts made by the bullmoose he was tracking. He was hungry. He hadn't eaten for three days and his last meal was merely a snowshoe rabbit, hardly enough to nourish him for long.

He followed the trail of the moose, keeping his nose into the wind. His prey would not pick up his scent as long as the wolf stayed downwind.

Except for the diamond-shaped cluster of white fur on his chest Midnight was totally black. He had not joined a wolf pack since he had run away from Miles Coffin. He had hunted alone and had tracked game relentlessly, crossing into many wolf territories, killing their game. He was a loner and did not honor accepted pack boundaries.

Game was not plentiful. The herds had thinned out and the wolf packs had killed off most of the old, the sick and the weak. They had buried what meat they didn't eat to sustain them over the lean months. Had Midnight been traveling with a pack he would have been privy to these frozen storehouses and would have had food to supplement those times when game was not available.

The scent of the bull moose was stronger now. Midnight was gaining on his prey. If the moose decided to stop and fight, once he realized Midnight was pursuing him, it would be a death struggle. Midnight did not welcome such an encounter in the deep, soft snow. The large, powerful moose could kill him or hurt him badly if the animal decided to stand his ground.

Midnight had left the shelter of the woods behind him and followed the great beast into a clearing. The freshly fallen snow shone a luminescent blue in the moonlight. It was deeper here but it was possible to track the moose. His were the only marks in the new covering. There was a small lake at the northwest corner of the clearing. It was frozen over. If he could chase the moose out onto the lake and kill him there he would have enough food for a long while.

The scent was stronger. The moose could not be far ahead of him. Midnight loped along, his shorter legs stretching at every leap to stay in the holes made by the moose's longer strides. Then, suddenly, about five hundred yards ahead, Midnight saw him. He was an immense male. Midnight's task would not be easy. The wolf's only chance for victory was if the moose was old, sick or that he would run.

The moose was heading in the direction of the lake and he apparently still didn't know he was being stalked. He was moving at a leisurely gait away from Midnight. He felt no peril for his life.

As Midnight drew closer, the beast ahead of him suddenly stopped in his tracks and threw his huge head in the air. He had picked up Midnight's scent and turned and faced the oncoming wolf who was only a few hundred yards away. In the clear light of the full moon, reflected in the blue-white snow, the moose stood perfectly still, staring out at the approaching menace, his head held high, his tremendous antlers cocked in defiance. He was not going to run.

There was hardly any vapor coming from the giant moose's nostrils, indicating that his lungs were not sickly and that he could sustain a battle. His long, sturdy legs held him well out of the snow, giving him the advantage over the wolf. His massive body weighed almost fourteen hundred pounds as compared to the wolf's one hundred and fifty pounds.

Midnight drew closer. When he was within thirty yards of the great beast he stopped. Their eyes met and locked. Not a sound was heard. They spoke to each other through their eyes. It was a message understood by each, a language that spoke of death. If the moose accepted his death by attack from the wolf he would turn and run. If he stood his ground it meant he rejected the wolf's demand on his life.

The moose stood immobile. He was ready to engage Midnight. The black wolf would not eat the moose's flesh tonight. He would not risk death when the battle's edge was not in his favor. There would be another day.

For fully five minutes the eyes of the two animals pored into each other's. This was no average moose. He had been in many battles and the marks of those conflicts were evident on his body. A long, ragged scar on his chest told of a savage goring by the antlers of another moose. The tips of three tines on his right antler had been broken off, leaving a jagged and deadly edge.

Midnight wisely loped away, retreating to the woods where he would survive on smaller meals until he came across more vulnerable game. Perhaps someday he would have another, more favorable meeting with this animal when the advantage would be his.

* * *

Midnight paused on a hill and hid in a cluster of birch trees and watched a small herd of caribou trek along the valley floor. The caribou came to drink at a stream that wound its way through the valley. The running water rarely froze over completely. It was a perfect spot for a kill. Midnight would have no trouble pursuing the caribou and taking one down. In places near the stream the snow had worn away, exposing the raw earth. Here he could run at a rapid pace with no difficulty.

Midnight could almost taste the sweet, pungent meat and his mouth began to water, saliva forming on his lips. In a few minutes he would no longer feel the pangs of hunger. And this meal would be satisfying, full.

He trotted out of the woods, keeping the wind in his favor, and worked his way down the long, sloping hill towards the small herd. They had paused at the stream and were drinking the cold, clear water when Midnight came into their peripheral view.

The caribou bolted at the sight of the great black wolf, his scent driving them into a frenzy. Midnight had already picked out his target. As the herd moved through the winding valley, the animal Midnight had singled out was having trouble breathing. Great gusts of vapor came from his nostrils in the cold thin air. His lungs were infected by parasites. As he trudged along in the white powder, the pounding of his body dropped spots of blood from his flesh. He was infested with winter ticks and would soon die in misery.

Midnight was on him easily. The single caribou had already fallen behind the herd. Midnight struck before his prey was into the deep powder. He leaped with a blinding speed and struck the animal with such force that he knocked it off its haunches and into the snow. The caribou lay on his side, his legs kicking out, as he struggled to right himself.

Midnight ran a few circles around the fallen animal, confusing him. Then he struck at the animal's head. His enormous incisor teeth bit through the caribou's nose and the powerful jaws crushed the bone. In minutes the large animal was dead from suffocation.

Midnight ripped out the soft underbelly of the fallen prey and buried his nose in the warm, wet meat. The smell was intoxicating. He tore out huge chunks of meat, swallowing some whole, savoring each mouthful. He had not eaten so well in weeks. The wolf's mighty jaws sought the ribs and cracked one off. He crunched it to get at the delicious marrow, a tasty end to his repast.

When Midnight was completely satiated he ripped large hunks of meat from the carcass and dragged them up a hill by a stand of pines. He dug out a hole in the hard ground with his paws and trudged back and forth to the carcass, burying each piece he carried. When he finished, he covered the hole and marked the surface to leave his scent. He could now return to his frozen storehouse in the future and find it without any trouble.

As Midnight started back down the hill he saw three ravens perched on the body, eating the remains. These birds often trailed wolf packs, hoping for the leftovers from a fresh kill. Midnight wasn't disturbed by their presence. He was willing to share with the large black birds.

When he got near the carcass the birds took off and landed on the upper limbs of a spruce tree, waiting there for Midnight to finish. But he was in no hurry. He sprawled out beside the caribou, mashing bones between his teeth. He felt no danger, even though wolf packs might be in the area, trailing the caribou herd.

Soon he drifted into a light slumber.

CHAPTER 4

Coffin had been on a predator control mission with a senior game biologist when he first met Lucy. He was working in an area close to the city of Juneau. The wolf population had grown tremendously over the seasons and professional hunters and wolfers had been hired to trim the wolf packs. In areas close to major cities there was no limit on the amount of wolves killed, but the authorities still liked to keep rein on the killing and not let the hunting turn into slaughter.

Coffin discovered that Lucy had been working in the Game and Fish Department for a year and they somehow had not crossed paths.

After they had become better acquainted he asked her, "How is it I never saw you around here?"

"Apparently you never looked," she quipped. "I've seen you though."

Thank God, he thought, that he had finally taken notice. She had been practically shoved in front of him. When he met her Lucy was directly involved with control of wolf population in most of the interior. Coffin's interest in wolves prompted her to meet him. She would have eventually, anyhow. Their paths were bound to cross.

She stood exactly a head shorter than him and she looked up into his eyes.

"Lucy Webb, meet Miles Coffin," the man standing beside them said.

Coffin took her hand in his but his eyes never parted from the gleaming intelligence that stared back at him.

"I hear you study wolves," she said.

"Sort of."

"Maybe we can work together sometime."

The first time Coffin took her out to his property he picked her up in Fairbanks at the local Game and Fish office. She was waiting for him in front of the building. It was a cold November day and she had the fur collar of her jacket pulled up around her face. How out of place she seemed in this environment, Coffin thought at the time. How fragile. The land was so overwhelmingly vast it diminished humanity. The slight woman seemed even more so.

Coffin stopped his Range Rover in front of her. She opened the door to get in. Her smiling face drastically changed to complete shock when she saw the large black wolf in the back seat.

"Oh, my God!" she exclaimed.

Coffin smiled. "Get in," he said warmly. "Don't be afraid. He won't harm you."

The wolf did not move. He sat immobile on the back seat, staring at Lucy. His green eyes burned, sending a chill through her body. She had never been afraid of animals, no matter their size. Even the largest, wildest dogs calmed in her presence. But there was a different sensation with this wolf. There was the sense of fantasy, almost a supernatural feeling about being with such a huge, strange, dangerous animal. He was completely black except for a diamond cluster of white fur on his chest.

"Come on," Coffin said. "Get in." She had not moved from her position in the doorway. Finally she braced herself and climbed in beside Coffin, absolutely fascinated by the wolf whose piercing eyes watched her.

Coffin reached back and roughly patted the wolf on the head. "This one is my pride at the moment," he said. "Say hello to Midnight."

"I've never met a wolf under such circumstances before," she stammered.

"Give him your hand, palm up," Coffin said.

"Will I get it back?"

Coffin smiled. "Go ahead," he said.

Lucy held out her hand and the wolf placed a giant paw in it. Lucy smiled weakly.

"I feel strange," she said. "Frightened and yet, I don't know. Exhilarated."

"See," Coffin said, smiling. "He already likes you."

When they arrived at Coffin's place he let the wolf out of the Range Rover. The animal stood alongside the vehicle, waiting to be led. Coffin took Lucy to the fenced area where he kept the small wolf pack. The animals were howling loudly at his return. As they drew near the eight-foot mesh wire fence that surrounded the area Lucy stopped and stared in amazement at the spectacle before her. Five wolves bunched at the gate howled their strange chilling cries of welcome. As she watched the wolves Lucy felt elemental, as if she too were a part of nature, merely just another animal. The wolves became playful and began romping and jumping on one another.

"We'll let them settle down some," Coffin said. "Then you can visit with them properly."

Lucy noticed the large black male had not left Coffin's side and had remained calm while the members of the pack were agitated.

"Coffin," Lucy said. "They're marvelous." She was truly entranced and was smiling.

Later he brought her cautiously into the pen. The wolves backed off and bowed in supplication. Some females tilted their heads to the side and exposed their necks to Coffin.

"They are accepting us," Coffin said. "They let us know they are submissive."

One female stepped back from the pack and lowered her front paws and head to the ground. She curled her black lips and snarled at Lucy.

"What's wrong?" Lucy asked. "Is he going to attack me?"

"No. She's a female. She's telling you she feels threatened by your presence. You are a new female in her world and she is the alpha female of the pack. She is challenging you."

"Oh," Lucy murmured. "What should I do?"

"Nothing. Just remain still."

Lucy froze at Coffin's command. The other wolves were crowding around her and Coffin. She had been around wolves before but she never felt so vulnerable as she did now.

Coffin called out to the wolves. "Stay!" he commanded.

The wolves squatted. The snarling female rose on her haunches and stared at Lucy. Lucy stepped forward and knelt on one knee before the wolf. The animal growled softly. Lucy extended her right arm and placed her hand on the animal's head.

"Lucy!" Coffin gasped, amazed that she showed no fear.

The wolf turned her head away from Lucy and exposed her neck to her. Lucy rubbed the offered spot gently. The wolf then began to nuzzle against her, becoming friendly.

"She won't harm me," Lucy said. "She's like a kitten."

Coffin took Lucy's arm and backed out of the pen. He locked the gate behind them. The wolves began to jostle each other once again.

"I'm sorry," Coffin said. "I should have let them get used to you first. I didn't expect her to be unfriendly."

"Would she really have attacked me?"

"I doubt it."

"Could you have handled them if something went wrong?"

"I wouldn't have taken you in there if I couldn't," Coffin answered.

*   *   *

Through the years Coffin had compiled many pages of notes and Lucy had urged him to produce a book on all they learned about wolves. He kidded her about it. He laughingly dubbed it "Confessions of a Former Wolf Hunter." Lucy did not share his mirth. She was serious about a manuscript.

There were times when the wolves were left alone on the property, times when both Coffin and Lucy had to leave on conservationist trips. During these periods they did not worry about the wolves breaking out and harming anyone in the area. There were no neighbors around for miles; the acreage was mostly solid woodland that blended into the surrounding wilderness.

Coffin often considered the possibility of Lucy's safety while he was away. Although the wolves accepted her as one of the pack, she was not looked upon as a leader. Rivalries always existed among the lesser wolves and one always tried to impose his will on another. Whenever Coffin was away he left a loaded .45 automatic with Lucy. Just in case.

Miles Coffin was born in Newfoundland in the tiny village of Come Again on the banks of Bonavista Bay. He spent the early part of his life engaged in the main occupation of his forebear, the inevitable fisherman. Faced with a future of eking out subsistence as a squid-jigger or dory fisherman, Coffin opted for a new life before he was twenty years old. He migrated to the mainland of Canada, held down a string of odd jobs and finally crossed the border into the United States. He settled in Boston for a few years while becoming a citizen of this great land of opportunity. At the peak of the Vietnam War he joined the U.S. Army and found himself locked in a conflict he didn't understand, fighting for his life in a place with a name as unfamiliar as his own birthplace. He fought side by side with men he hardly knew for two terrible years, motivated only by survival, and was exposed for the first time in his young life to the brutal violence he later came to believe was common in all mankind.

Confused in mind and spirit, Coffin took his discharge after the Army and once again drifted from job to job. In Anchorage, Alaska he finally ceased his aimless journey and welcomed that last great frontier as the refuge he sought to stem his wanderlust. He took to the wilderness immediately, finding the overwhelming size of the territory the perfect retreat to search for purpose in his aimless life.

In the early nineteen-seventies Miles Coffin found his forte as a hunting guide. Coffin conducted parties which brought down moose, elk, deer, bear and wolves. In those days the restrictions on wolves that were to later emerge did not exist. The wolf was fair game in unlimited quantities. Considered a predator, hated and feared by man, the wolf was killed with complete impunity in a reckless determination to obliterate his species. The change in Coffin's outlook came with a series of incidents involving the ruthless killing of these animals. On an expedition conducted specifically to rout a wolf pack that had grown to thirty members and had drastically reduced game around their territory, Coffin saw himself as a man without honor.

Coffin had led the group of hunters in three small airplanes. They cut the wolf pack off from shelter and they ripped the wolves to shreds with repeated bursts from shotguns. It was the memory of the animals in the snow, their bodies wrecked and splayed across the blood-spattered surface and the loathing of the hunters who laughed at the efforts of the dying animals to continue running that irrevocably turned Coffin against the senseless slaughter.

After years of pointless carnage Coffin finally found some purpose in his life. He vowed to use his time to study and understand the nature of the wolf. He no longer participated in wholesale slaughter. He practiced and promoted restraint. As a guide, he insisted on the barest minimum kills.

Coffin finally married at the age of forty-eight. His wife was younger by fifteen years. When Lucy Webb first met Miles Coffin the furthest thought from her mind was becoming his wife. He was not, by most standards, the kind of man women dream about.

Tall and lank, with a rawboned spareness, he had the look of a man as out of place indoors as a pine tree. He even had the smell of the forest about him. His face was lined and carved by the wind and his short beard and long hair were streaked with gray. He moved with an awkward energy, leaning slightly forward when he walked, like the action of a snapped whip. He had about him the essence of the animals with whom he spent so much time.

He dressed in clothing made to suit his environment. A suit did not exist in his wardrobe. He was a throwback to the pioneers who first came to the Alaska wilderness. He wore a fur-lined hide jacket, heavy corduroy pants, tucked into knee-high boots.

Lucy Webb was thirty-three years old when Miles Coffin asked her to marry him. At first the difference in their ages worried her. Lucy was surprised and pleased to learn that Coffin did not think of himself as a forty-eight-year-old man. He had strength and stamina coupled with a drive for sex and work that was, if anything, tiring for her. His appetite for lovemaking was greater than her own and he satisfied it with an animal-like intensity.

Lucy spent a happy, if somewhat sheltered life, growing up in her parents' Victorian house near Seattle. As a child she developed an active affection for animals. She brought home stray kittens, dogs, injured birds. She fed them and cared for their wounds. She was happiest in the presence of animals. Her father said she preferred them to humans.

She was a natural for the job she held.

Their interest in the creatures of the wild was common ground for a relationship. He, like her, was against the senseless slaughter of animals. Lucy worked within the confines of the rules set by the government. Coffin made his own rules.

Together, they raised wolves on the property Coffin had purchased years before. They nurtured and sheltered the animals, keeping no more than a small pack of six wolves at a time. Through the early years of their marriage they sealed a common bond. They learned much about the misunderstood animal. They observed the close family ties of the wolf to members of his litter, their loyalty, their ability to communicate, their stamina, affection and, remarkably, their flair for social order.

They found that wolves did not make ideal household pets once they matured. They longed for the life and social functions of the pack. They lived to hunt and when that ability was withdrawn the wolf eventually withered into mere replicas of the proud animals they were destined to become. Man, Coffin decided, could not truly domesticate the wolf. He was, after all, a wild animal by his nature. He could be tamed and his fear of man could be quelled, but he could never be integrated into a human environment for a sustained period without ultimately rebelling or having his spirit destroyed. One thing Coffin and Lucy had learned about the wolves was that they were independent animals with a need to live in the wilderness and hunt for food. In captivity, the wolf could never live normally. He had to live in the wild as a hunter to function and survive in the social order of the pack.

When each new litter grew to maturity Coffin and his wife set the wolves free. He took each one individually into the interior and let them integrate into a natural environment. New litters were again studied, cared for and brought to maturity. Coffin developed a respect for the wolf brought on by his intense desire to atone for the killings in his earlier years. He no longer pictured the wolf as a thing of evil, to be scorned and hated. Coffin thought of the wolf as a noble animal with integrity as great as any highly regarded wild animal.

* * *

Coffin had expanded the house since he and Lucy were married. Their combined effort had taken a few years and had increased the size from a four-room structure to more than double its original size. He had let the wolves roam inside the house when they were pups. But he moved them into the fenced area as they matured and were ready to accept social order. Coffin knew he had made a mistake trying to domesticate Midnight. The wolf had been obstinate. He dominated the members of the pack. He had a tendency to fight. In the wild he would undoubtedly make a good leader in a large pack, but the confined space of the pen did not satisfy him.

How could he have been so wrong, Coffin thought. How could he have not realized sooner that Midnight would harm Lucy? The signs were there all along. He ruled the pack by fear. He dominated and controlled them by intimidation. They were afraid of him. Coffin knew that. Why didn't he see what Midnight was truly capable of?

His memories of Lucy tormented him now. They were constantly in his mind. Every conscious minute was filled with images he would never forget. On his return from one of his expeditions, as he neared their log-cabin, he heard the howling of the wolves who were penned on the property. They knew he was back. Their cries were of approval. The lights of the cabin sparkled like jewels in the black night. As he came closer he saw Lucy silhouetted by the light of the open front door. She had been watching his headlight approach through the woods.

"I missed you," she had softly said.

"The feeling is mutual," Coffin told her.

"Are you hungry?" she asked.

"You bet."

"I'll throw on a steak."

"Afterwards," he said, his face breaking into a broad grin. "I'm hungrier for you."

Afterwards Coffin lay next to her in bed. He was naked on his back. A small glass ashtray rested on his flat stomach while he smoked a cigarette. He watched the gray smoke curl slowly towards the ceiling making misty patterns against the hand-hewn logs that stretched across the width of the room. He had cut the logs from pine trees behind the cabin. He remembered the effort he had put into building the small log house.

He crushed out the butt in the ashtray and placed it on an end table. He rolled over on top of Lucy and buried his head between her breasts.

"God," he said. "There is nothing as beautiful as a woman's body. Let's go at it again."

She rolled away from his grasp. "Oh no. First you eat. Then we'll see how frisky you feel later. We've got all the time in the world."

All the time in the world. How damned ironic that simple statement sounded now. He had watched her that evening as she left his bed and dressed herself. Desire had flooded his brain. He wondered then how he had survived for so many years without her. She was a small, slim woman with small, fully rounded breasts. Her long, blonde hair fell over her shoulders and she tossed it carelessly aside as she slipped into a plaid shirt. The face beneath the yellow hair was more angular than oval, high cheekbones giving a permanent uplift to the corners of her mouth. It was a pleasant face, Coffin thought, exuding the pleasure of enjoying her life.

The memory of his love made him shudder with grief.

CHAPTER 5

Coffin shipped Lucy's body back to Seattle to her parents for burial. He could not go with her. The overwhelming guilt he felt for her sudden death kept him from facing her family. He knew he was responsible for the wolves' attack on her and he damned himself for his complicity.

Had she never met him she would be alive today, probably happily married with a few kids. What had she gotten from her time with him? He had given her only a couple of years of reclusive hard work that would have eventually sapped the life out of her.

And for what? His lifestyle. Not hers. He never considered what she wanted. She simply followed him. He accepted the leadership role, became the alpha male, never questioned it, and led her inevitably to her death. It was his fault she died. She never handled a weapon; didn't consider guns a part of her life. And he knew this. She wouldn't have thought of taking the .45 automatic into the pen to protect herself. She could not kill the wolves. She would never have pulled the trigger on any one of them. She would have tried to calm the wolves, soothe them, talk to them. Shoot them? Never.

And he knew that.

Lucy had never been involved in controlling a wolf pack. Coffin brought her into direct contact with the wolves he maintained. Lucy had led a sheltered life, while his was filled with violence and death. Her entire life was one of gentleness and caring. She cared for animals while Coffin manipulated them.

With his acceptance of guilt, Coffin realized facts about himself he had never admitted before. Did he have an ultimate purpose in keeping wolves and guiding their destiny? Did he feel remorse for destroying so many wolves earlier in his life? Was he now offering his life as atonement?

He was completely lost and confused. He existed without purpose. He was beyond loneliness; he was totally depressed. How could he face a future without Lucy? The tremendous weight of sorrow was unbearable and impossible to avoid.

He sat in the living room of the cabin with a photo of Lucy. It was taken at their wedding. Coffin loved the picture. Her smile and bright, intelligent eyes were the essence of the woman he loved. He set the photo down on the coffee table beside his .45 automatic. His hand drifted to the gun and his fingers closed around it. He lifted it slowly, his mind dazed, clouded by the picture of Lucy. He placed the gun at his temple and pulled the trigger. The hammer fell dead with a hollow click. He had not thrown a round into the chamber.

He dropped the gun on the table. The loud clatter shocked him to reality. He had subconsciously just committed suicide. Was that what he wanted? Was that the only course left?

"Damn it!" he swore. "Damn my life!"

He got up from the table and wandered outside to the pen. He started inside but could not go to where Lucy had died. It would only add torture to the misery he felt. He walked to the garage. Inside were the Range Rover and a jeep. He thought of sealing the garage doors, getting behind the seat and letting the motor run. Put an end to it. Instead, he climbed the stairs to the loft and found himself looking out the windows at the fenced compound below. Visions of the horror that had happened in that area raced through his mind. He turned abruptly away and knocked the video camera off its moorings. He grabbed the tripod before it hit the floor. A swift reaction had saved it from damage. What the hell difference did it make if it was damaged? He didn't care about anything.

He set the camera and tripod down and walked away. Halfway down the stairs an image flashed in his mind. The tape in the camera had run out. He went back and snapped it out of the camera. It was at its end. He had not used the camera since before he had left Lucy alone. Could she have taped the wolves? During the storm?

He went back to the house and put the tape into the VCR. He rewound it to the beginning and turned it on. Not much showed. Routine footage of the wolves. He fast-forwarded the tape, racing through material that he and Lucy had already compiled. Suddenly, the images were different. He was looking at the ice storm. A couple of wolves huddled near the fence. The fallen tree lay on the lean-to, part of which was crushed.

Lucy stepped into the frame. Coffin's body shivered with fear for her. He almost cried out to her. He watched her chip at the ice on the lock and step inside the fence. The flashlight in her hand gave enough light for the camera to pick up decent, if not clear, images. Lucy went into the lean-to and came out, the flashlight searching for the wolves she sought to help.

The beam of light fell fully on Midnight, who was no more than ten or twelve feet from her. He was crouched in an attack mode and ready to spring. It happened so fast Coffin was not prepared. The huge black wolf catapulted through the air and took Lucy to the ground. The flashlight flew from her hand to the ground, its beam defining the action. Midnight ripped at her throat and she was lifeless in an instant. The big wolf backed off and other members of the pack attacked the fallen woman and ripped at her.

Coffin crushed his temples with his hands and cried out.

"Midnight! You damned beast! You! It was you! Why? Why?"

The tape continued to run. As the wolves were occupied with Lucy's body Midnight ran directly at the fence, vaulted to the top and scrambled down the other side.

Coffin grabbed the .45 from the table, snapped a round into the chamber and fired at the tv screen. It blew apart in a shower of smoke and sparks.

"You will die for this, wolf," Coffin shouted. "I swear to you. You will die."

CHAPTER 6

He was in wolf pack territory.

Miles Coffin eased the stick forward and let the Piper Cub settle gently on the soft headwind which floated up through the ridges of tall spruce rimming the valley below. He held the small plane steadily with one hand and tossed a spent cigarette out the open window to his left. As the plane dipped lower he cradled a loaded shotgun in his lap.

He knew this valley well and just how the plane would handle on the early spring winds. He had guided the Piper to many landings in this part of the Alaska interior. The cold wind brushed the gray hairs of his short beard. He glanced out the window at the familiar face of the rugged country. It seemed not so long ago he was looking down at this same terrain in the role of wolf hunter. Most of the wolfers operated their planes with two men, the pilot and the man who did the shooting from the passenger seat. Coffin had alternated many times as either pilot or trigger man. Now, alone in the small craft, he was prepared to function simultaneously in both roles. He was hunting Midnight. His life had narrowed to one purpose: to kill the black wolf. He had come alone because he wanted no one with him who might interfere with his resolve, no matter how long it took. It was months since Lucy's death and Coffin had followed the trail of the black wolf through leads given to him by many of the people he worked with over the years, both officials of the state and hunters who claimed they had spotted the black wolf.

Wolf packs were defenseless against attack from an airplane and, invariably, they were slaughtered. Killing the wolves was easy. The hunters flew over a pack, getting down as low as ten feet above the snow-packed ground. The trick was to catch a pack in the open, a feat not difficult to accomplish, since most wolves were always on the move. The buzzing plane would frighten the wolves, driving them into a frenzy. The triggerman in the passenger seat fired out of the open window and cut down the slower moving wolves from above. The plane would fly over them in a little circle and come back to administer another dose of sudden, swift death.

Hunting wolves by plane or helicopter was strictly outlawed in the state of Alaska and the penalties for breaking this particular law were severe; a heavy fine, possible jail sentence and even confiscation of the airplane. Coffin knew the costs if he was caught. Although he needed his plane to reduce the vast distances he traveled, in his present state of mind, he was willing to take his chances. The possibility of not getting caught was in his favor. It would be difficult to prove that he had hunted the wolves by plane. The bodies of the wolves he killed would be eaten by predators and covered over by storms.

Flying low over the landscape, Coffin was wolf hunter once again. All the effort he had put into learning the habits of wolves was useful now to assist him in hunting and killing them. He had become heartless, a more calculated hunter than he once was, determined to annihilate every wolf he encountered while he had life in him. He directed the hatred he felt not just to Midnight but to all wolves.

Coffin spotted a wolf pack strung out, single-file, running in the snow. As he flew in low over them to get a better look, he felt a jolt of exhilaration. There, in the third position, was a large black wolf running with the pack. It could be Midnight, he thought. It was impossible to tell, flying swiftly above the wolves. He circled the pack, came in lower and straight at the column. He was no more than twenty feet off the ground as he zoomed over them. He kept his sight on the black wolf, trying to determine if it was indeed Midnight. But he saw no white on the wolf's chest. He couldn't be sure. He was passing over too quickly. He banked and came in for another low run. It was then that he realized that it didn't matter to him at all if the wolf was Midnight. He didn't care. He was going to kill it anyhow.

He dipped the plane low to the left so that he could get a clear shot at the wolves without hitting any parts of the plane. He rested the barrel on the window edge and maneuvered the slide-action shotgun with his right hand while guiding the plane with the other. Many a triggerman had caused a crash by knocking out lines or ripping away portions of the plane's skis with a bad shot. But Coffin was accomplished enough to avoid such a mishap even though he would be shooting while flying.

The shotgun barked and a wolf dropped in the snow below, its feet kicking as it died. On the next swing over the pack, Coffin dropped a bit lower, coming within a few feet of the ground. The plane roared over the heads of the pack, frightening them, and breaking their single file. The wolves bunched up and would now make better targets than the stretched-out line which was more their habit. The pack's lesser wolves automatically followed the lead wolf. They were running at full speed on the hard, frozen snow as the plane passed over them again. Coffin pumped a fresh cartridge into the chamber and opened fire. Another wolf dropped as the gun exploded. The black wolf was still running in the cluster of wolves. Coffin was very low and could almost see the fear in their eyes as they tried vainly to escape him.

The wolves looked up at him as he passed over. They were panicking now and running for their lives away from the sound of booming death. They separated from the lead wolf and fanned out, each going in a different direction. Coffin watched the black wolf cut his own trail through the snow. He banked in a tight circle and came around behind the black wolf. He abandoned the shotgun. It was cumbersome to handle while still keeping control of the plane. He hefted the loaded .45 automatic in his left hand and held it out the open window.

He came in low, keeping the wolf to his left. He waited until he was close enough to make the bullets count. When he was almost on him he opened up. The .45 barked and the big animal stumbled and rolled over in the snow. Coffin had dropped him.

When he guided the plane for a landing the wolves had completely dispersed. He settled the Piper Cub down gently on the smooth surface and glided on the skis until he felt he was as close as he could get without taking a chance with the fallen wolf. He cut the motor about twenty feet from the wolf, climbed out of the plane with the pistol held at arm's length. As he got closer to the wolf it struggled to get to its feet. The animal was still alive.

Closer yet he saw it wasn't Midnight. There was no patch of white fur on the chest. He aimed at the center of the animal and fired twice. The wolf slumped forward in the snow, dead.

"That settles your hide," Coffin spat at the dead wolf. "You'll never kill anyone."

*   *   *

Miles Coffin waited patiently on the high ground for the mule deer to show himself. He had watched the six-pointed stag through binoculars for over an hour. Coffin kept himself low to the ground and out of the line of view. The deer traveled with two females, stopping to feed on saplings along their route in high grass. They were coming toward him, moving steadily up the ridge where he perched at the crest.

Coffin made no sudden moves, keeping as still as humanly possible, while the deer came slowly into range. Any quick move, even a shift of the wind, might spook the deer and set him off in the wrong direction. The deer moved up the slope, seeking higher ground.

The hunter lifted his Winchester M-70 carefully from the hard, rocky ground and settled the stock into his shoulder. He aimed, quickly framing his prey in the telescopic sight. He caressed the trigger until the target was aligned perfectly, then squeezed off a round. The deer stumbled and dropped from the impact of the slug that ripped through its hindquarters and shattered bone and sinew.

A perfect shot from over three hundred yards. The does bolted and leaped down the hill in long bounds. Coffin was not interested in their flight. He slung the rifle over his shoulder and scrambled down the long slope.

When he got to the spot where the stag had gone down he was surprised to find that the animal was still alive. It was lying on its left side, its front legs kicking furiously in an effort to right itself. The right hind leg was blown away. Coffin stepped up to the deer and slipped his rifle from his shoulder. He pointed the barrel at the animal's heart. The deer was a young male. His antlers did not extend very far from where they joined his skull. The sacrificial animal, Coffin thought. It would provide food to keep Coffin alive and bait to draw a wolf pack.

The animal turned his head and looked up at his slayer. His woeful eyes held a plea that vanished in an instant as the rifle exploded and the slug burst his heart apart.

Coffin cleaned out the deer's innards and sliced sections of meat. He was sure of one thing; he would not starve in the wilderness. Game was plentiful for an armed hunter. When he finished he left the carcass for the wolves who would come for the meat of the dead deer. They would inevitably follow the ravens who would lead them to the meat.

Coffin waited, hidden in a stand of pines on the high ground, until a wolf pack showed itself, his finger resting on the trigger. He had formed a dugout around himself from broken branches and pine needles. It had gotten colder but new snow had not fallen for a few days. The sun kept the temperature slightly higher during the day. But it was starting to cloud up as the evening settled in. It would snow soon and he would have to seek protection in the thick forest. Staying alive in the severe cold was the greatest problem facing him. Coffin had lived outdoors during winter months and he knew the danger. Sooner or later, he would have to face a decision; he could not stay out here indefinitely and hope to remain healthy. But he truly didn't care.

He kept a small fire going inside the makeshift lean-to. The heat from a fire was necessary for a man to live. He constantly massaged his hands and feet even though he was covered with the best winter gear he could find.

He fell asleep. His mind filled with happy images of Lucy as he dreamed. Lucy laughing. Lucy happy. Lucy in bed with him, his arms smothering her with his love. And into this happy vision came the menacing shadow of the large black wolf. It charged. Midnight. Straight for Lucy's throat. Ripping her. Killing her.

He awoke with a jolt. Lucy was dead. Dead and gone forever. Nothing could ever change that.

Something moved down below where he had left the slain deer. It was almost nightfall, on the edge of dusk. Long shadows lined the snow. The fire had died. Only a few embers still smoldered. Coffin rubbed his eyes and brought them into focus. Yes. Something moved near the dead animal. He couldn't make out what it was. It looked like the shape of a wolf. But there should be more than one. A pack. Unless it was a lone wolf.

The shape took form as his eyes adjusted to the dim light. Damn, he thought. Why did he have to fall asleep now? He squinted. It was a wolf. The shape was large and dark. Midnight?

The wolf moved cautiously around the deer, sensing danger. Coffin grasped his rifle and jammed it to his shoulder. He sighted through the telescopic sight and brought the wolf into focus. It looked like Midnight. He couldn't see if there was a patch of white on the animal's chest because it was bent over. Could he be so lucky? Could it be Midnight?

Suddenly the wolf bolted. Coffin fired. He thought he hit him, but he wasn't sure. The wolf disappeared as the ground dropped off. Coffin tried to find him in his sight. He saw movement and fired again. But the wolf was gone. Into the shadows and into the dark forest below where the deer lay.

Damn, Coffin swore. He had dozed off and lost his chance. It could have been Midnight. The wolf was large enough. Coffin got to his feet and tried to spot the wolf. But the light was almost gone. He couldn't even make out the tracks in the snow. He climbed back to the shelter of the lean-to and rebuilt the fire. Sleep. He would start fresh in the morning and follow the wolf's tracks in the daylight. There was nothing he could do at night.

In the morning he broke camp and followed the trail left by the lone wolf. It led him into the dense woods where he lost it in the rough terrain. The wolf could have gone in any direction. It was impossible to track him unless he got lucky. If it was Midnight, alone, he might continue moving for hundreds of miles. A lone wolf never stuck to a territory until a pack accepted him. For now he had lost the wolf.

*   *   *

Coffin and the wilderness were one.

He was like the lone wolf. With one difference. He survived to kill. The wolf killed as part of the natural order of survival of the fittest. Coffin's absorption into the great wilderness was a decision to pursue and kill one acknowledged foe: the great black wolf. He, unlike the wolf, did not care what happened to him as long as his mission was accomplished. The wolf cared about his future and the future of his pack.

Coffin, by now, accepted no social order. He functioned outside the limits of his own society and did not care how he achieved his goal. So far, in the months he spent hunting Midnight, he lost count of the wolves he had killed.

He wondered where his obsession would lead him.

CHAPTER 7

Moon was a pure white female wolf, the anomaly of the pack with whom she had spent the first two years of her life. She weighed eighty-five pounds and was of average height and weight for a female her age. It was only her blinding white fur that distinguished her from the other wolves. She was intelligent and loyal. She was destined to become one of the prime females and she would be relegated to the position of mating with the lead wolf.

Moon watched Smoke, a large gray wolf, as he led the pack over the crest of a hill at the timber line. He was the alpha male of the wolf pack, the undisputed leader. He was the largest male in the pack, which numbered nineteen. He weighed close to one hundred and twenty pounds.

The wolves had been following a flock of ravens for two days and nights. The large black birds would eventually lead them to game but the winter had been unusually fierce and the hunting lean. Only nine males and four females actually hunted, while the remainder of the wolves stayed behind in their lairs.

The wolves followed Smoke over the hill and into the valley below. They stayed in a tight group with Smoke as the spearhead.

They carved a path in the snow, pointing down the valley like an arrow, relentlessly forging ahead toward their goal.

The wolves hunted within the accepted boundaries of their own territory, defined by scent posts. These marks were made by urinating in spots, leaving their own scent as an indication to other packs that it was dangerous to cross. Game that migrated through these imaginary boundaries was theirs to kill. Once prey left their territory Smoke and the members of his pack honored the boundaries that joined theirs and did not pursue game into that region.

Smoke and his hunters covered long distances to find food. They traveled days at a time, literally hundreds of miles, as they patrolled the perimeters of their boundaries, doubling back many times and crossing their own trails. Smoke's pack patrolled an area of over three hundred square miles. They would defend these boundaries to the death, as would neighboring packs, for their established grounds.

Smoke had picked up the scent of a caribou herd over a mile to the north, well within the confines of their hunting grounds, but they would have to hurry to catch them. He pressed harder, urging the pack on, as they crashed through the snow.

*   *   *

Midnight lay in the sun, lightly napping while he digested his recent feast. He had moved up a hill to a ridge, away from what remained of his kill, watching the three ravens pick at the carcass. His eyes were half closed and he viewed the birds with only a cursory interest. As he drifted into a gentle sleep his olfactory senses told him something was amiss. His eyes snapped open. He had picked up the scent of the wolves into whose boundaries he had strayed. He recognized the scent from their droppings and he became instantly alert to this new danger.

He surveyed the terrain. He saw the pack led by a large gray wolf descending the slope to the valley floor. Midnight sensed they had been on his trail and had already seen him. He stood to

his full height and stretched his limbs, angry that his brief inter-
lude with sleep had been interrupted. He was ready to engage in
mortal combat if necessary. He was not going to run from the
wolves.

*   *   *

A new scent reached Smoke's nostrils and the members of the
pack. It was mixed with the smell of freshly killed caribou. It was
strong, distinctively isolated from the other. It was the scent of a
wolf, not one of his pack. It came from none of the neighboring
packs either. It could only be a lone wolf who had strayed into
their territory and had made a kill.

Smoke came out of the woods, his horde close behind. He
stopped at the edge of the clearing. Below, in the valley, by the
edge of the stream, was the remains of the caribou Midnight had
killed. The three ravens, who led the pack to the kill site, were still
ripping at fragments of flesh.

Smoke viewed the surrounding landscape, his eyes following
the tracks Midnight had left on the opposite valley wall. Finally he
saw Midnight. The huge black wolf was halfway up the hill across
the river near a clump of pine, standing still and waiting. Smoke
howled and led the pack down the hill in a mad charge. The interloper must be driven off.

*   *   *

Midnight stood his ground at the crest of the hill with the
thicket of pines behind him. The pack would be forced to attack
him from the front and would have a difficult time surrounding
him.

He watched as the gray wolf led the pack across the river bed
until they drew near the carcass of the fallen caribou. The ravens
sensed a violent confrontation was about to occur and took off for
a higher, safe perch.

The lead wolf halted at the foot of the hill, his green eyes fixed on Midnight. The decision had to be made quickly. Fight the intruder, risk injury, or pursue the caribou whose scent told him they were only a short distance from where the pack paused. The remaining members of the pack needed food. The interloper could wait.

Smoke turned away from Midnight and directed his followers in a rapid gait along the river bed in the direction the small herd of caribou had gone.

Midnight watched the pack fade from his view, but his eyes could not stray from the magnificent white female who trailed closely behind the lead gray wolf. She drew him on.

*   *   *

The caribou had slowed. They no longer felt threatened by the presence of more wolves since one of their herd had already fallen. The buck who had died was sick and would only have been a hardship on the herd. They relaxed and moved at a much slower pace, already tired from the chase.

Suddenly, at their heels, as if from nowhere, came a pack of hungry wolves, charging through the snow. The caribou bolted in unison, realizing the danger, and set out once more at a run. But the wolves were upon them. Smoke and his pack were not to be denied this time. They caught up to the herd quickly and took down two animals, leaving the rest of the herd to escape.

*   *   *

Midnight watched from a shelter of thick spruce as the wolf pack led by the gray male gorged themselves on the flesh of the caribou. Mostly he watched Moon as she buried her head in the open wounds of a fallen animal, tearing out and devouring huge chunks of meat. Midnight hid in the shelter of the trees and waited until the wolves were finished. Then he followed them as they left the remains of the prey and headed south.

Midnight followed for miles before he finally made a move against the wolves. As the pack rounded an abutment they were suddenly confronted by the huge black wolf who blocked their progress.

Smoke stopped the pack. His eyes locked with Midnight's while neither wolf moved. Swiftly Smoke charged the bold wolf who challenged him. There was no avoiding a fight this time. Smoke felt the threat at their first meeting.

Midnight stood defiantly in the pack's path of progress. He was daring Smoke and the pack to fight. It was to be a death struggle for leadership. The black wolf would become the new leader of the pack if he could defeat Smoke and subjugate the other members to his will. If he won the fight and succeeded in dominating them, they would accept him.

Midnight was heavier than Smoke by thirty pounds and was broader in the chest and shoulders. His head was larger, indicating more powerful jaws and larger canine teeth. But Smoke was quick and was an experienced fighter. He felt no fear and his first charge took the black wolf by surprise. Smoke collided with Midnight, knocking him off balance and spinning him around. Smoke tore a small chunk of fur and flesh from Midnight's chest on their first contact.

As Smoke circled the black wolf, Midnight responded with blinding speed. He lunged at his opponent so quickly that the pack was stunned. Midnight's jaws caught Smoke by the throat as his body crashed into the gray wolf. The force of his weight turned Smoke completely around and spun him off balance. Midnight's powerful grip tore the gray wolf's throat open in one ripping motion and the struggle was over in an instant. Smoke never had a chance against the stronger, more determined black wolf.

With the fallen wolf dying in the snow beside him, his blood staining the trampled surface, Midnight turned and faced the pack. They had recovered from the shock of witnessing their leader's sudden death and were moving on Midnight, closing around him in a wide circle.

Midnight did not let them attack. He picked out the largest of the males and struck at him before the pack could close the circle. He hit the wolf with his forepaws extended and knocked him off balance. With a quick burst of speed, Midnight was immediately on the stunned wolf. He ripped open the wolf's vulnerable underbelly and left him kicking in the snow.

Midnight now confronted the remaining wolves. Moon had stopped in her tracks. She stood immobile. She was awed by the ferocity of this huge, beautiful black wolf who had challenged the entire pack. Two wolves were dying and he was ready to continue his assault. If they all rushed him at once most likely they would kill him. But that would not be. The wolves needed a leader to make the motion to attack. They stopped advancing on Midnight who stood his ground. They were very cautious of this highly combative male.

Midnight chose his next victim, and, rather than lunging at him, he approached slower, head to head, keeping alert to any sudden moves by the other wolves. He growled at the wolf, a direct challenge to fight. The wolf fell to the ground and rolled over on his back in the snow, exposing his underbelly to Midnight in a gesture of complete supplication. Midnight turned to the next wolf and he too rolled onto his back as had the other. A few more followed. They, in turn, would not fight Midnight. They had accepted him as alpha animal. None would contest his victory or his dominance over them.

Midnight strolled to the superb white female who had drawn him to the pack. Moon stood perfectly still, her paws rooted in the snow. Midnight could not contain himself. He thrust his nose forward, nuzzling it under her ears, sniffing her body. He rooted his muzzle around her nose, mouth, under her belly, at her anus, along her legs until he was totally consumed with her scent. The other wolves watched, seeing the reason for Midnight's attack on the lead wolf come to fruition.

Midnight began playfully nudging Moon with his nose and head. He rubbed along the surface of her shoulders and caressed her under the ears with his tongue. He gently closed his mouth around her muzzle in a soft bite.

He had chosen her as his mate. Moon finally turned her head and nuzzled her nose into the thick black fur of this fierce, courageous animal. She accepted him also as her mate.

CHAPTER 8

In the spring, Moon had a litter of five pups. Not one looked like her or Midnight. They were all gray and could have been the offspring of any one of the wolves in the pack.

Moon spent her time nursing and cleaning her newborn pups, urging them to draw milk from her while keeping them warm and safe. They lived in a lair that was dug out under the roots of a very old spruce. It was high on a hill that looked out on a clearing a mile across at its widest point. The entrance was narrow, wide enough only for one adult to enter. Moon kept the tiny cave and her pups extremely clean at all times. Disease and infection could rob her of half her litter if she did not attend to them constantly.

Since the pack had accepted Midnight as their alpha animal, he spent most of his time leading the subordinate wolves on constant forays for meat. With the death of Smoke most of the pack easily gave in to Midnight's assertion. He had trouble with only two of the more aggressive lower-ranking males whom he fought and drove off. These males had caused the pack to split, taking with them members of their immediate family.

With Midnight as their leader, the pack now consisted of twelve adults and Snow's new pups, totaling seventeen. The fearful winter had continued well into April and food was scarce. The old and sickly members of the deer herds had long since died off. The remaining deer were healthy and they easily eluded the wolves in the deep snow. Only on rare occasions was Midnight able to return with a goodly portion of meat to his new family. Meat from large kills were stored in the pack's warehouses. These helped them survive when only small game was to be found.

Midnight adapted quickly to pack life. He was a natural leader. He made the transition to responsible member of a wolf pack with no difficulty. His true nature as a social animal emerged.

Hunting improved in the warmer months that followed. Midnight proved to be an even more resourceful leader than Smoke. The pack fared better overall under Midnight's reign. He expanded the pack's territory.

Midnight taught the quickly growing pups the ways of survival in the wilderness. Of the five pups born, there were four males and one female. One male pup was withdrawn and shied away from the rough and tumble antics of his brothers and sister. He would eventually become sickly and would be a drain on the pack. He had to be done away with before he got much older.

Two other males became inseparable. They jostled and tumbled one another constantly and were always found in each other's company. They even slept together, drawing warmth from each other's body. Their puppy-like antics continued into the summer. Quite the contrary with the fifth pup. He, like Midnight, had immediately revealed his dominance of the other pups. By the time he was six weeks old he made it a common occurrence to assert his dominance of his brothers by gently gripping their muzzles in his jaws and forcing them to the ground into submission. On hunting trips with his sire, he proudly trailed close behind Midnight with his head held high, almost touching the larger wolf's outstretched tail.

The female was the most curious of the litter. Her curiosity became a sore spot for her parents. They were constantly dragging her back to the lair, her bad habits leading her into all kinds of risky situations. Once, she was found trying to climb a wall of rock to an eagle's nest to get at the young birds. Luckily Moon got to her before the mother eagle did. This drawback to her nature subsided as she grew older and her aggressiveness turned in her favor on the hunt. She loved being in the middle of the chase and the kill, running alongside her father, mother and brothers.

As the summer wore on, the pups became proficient and were able to join the elders on many expeditions for food, assisting in ambushes. The sickly male pup faltered many times and fell behind. He had become epileptic. Midnight killed the pup by crushing his muzzle and smothering him.

During the early summer Moon and Midnight lost one other pup. The two inseparable male pups were romping carelessly near the lair. In the excitement of their activity, one of the pups rolled down a hill into a small gully. The young wolf did not return. The other pup went into a frenzy. He raced around the area outside the lair hysterically howling for the pack to find his favorite brother. The wolves never found the unfortunate pup. He had probably been stolen by a large predator; possibily an eagle, for the wolves would have sensed an animal on the ground near their lair. The lesson his playmate learned was never forgotten. Always would he be on the alert to the constant dangers which surrounded him.

* * *

By the end of summer the pack numbered fifteen. The three remaining pups were almost fully grown and accompanied the other members on practically every hunt. They would not possess the maturity to be true hunters for at least another year. The pack patrolled the outer boundaries of their territory every day. Sometimes the pack covered hundreds of miles in one day. Mostly they hunted at night because the scent of the prey was easier to detect at that time. They relied on their keen sense of smell and sight to find game, but sometimes their constant companions, the ravens, would lead them to a herd of caribou. Their determination and dogged perseverance spelled the difference between survival and extinction.

The spiral of life for the wolf had continued for millions of years and would repeat uninterrupted had not the wolves' one living enemy, man, made his appearance.

Midnight was the only member to know man. Soon after he ran from Miles Coffin, he had been tracking a mule deer when he heard a deafening explosion that stopped him in his tracks. It was a weapon of man that barked out death. When the fright passed, he found a fallen deer, dead in the snow. He had cautiously drawn near. Suddenly the deafening explosion rang out again and he felt a sharp pain in his right ear. Instantly, he bolted away from the deer as the loud noise followed again. A puff of snow exploded beside him. He ran off into the night, lucky to escape with his life.

It was as he had remembered when he was in captivity. Wherever man was, animals died. Midnight sensed that the noise the man made had somehow hurt him. The man meant to kill him. From then on he made a wide detour of man whenever he encountered him.

Midnight could not tell of his encounter with the hunter to the pack. He could only lead them away from the dangers of man. They were in a forest and were just coming into a glade when they detected a foreign scent. Midnight immediately recognized it as man and he directed them back the way they had come. The pack left the area, circling wide to the north. When they came out of the woods, above the men, they were upwind of them and did not pick up their scent as they moved back into the clearing. The hunters had been hidden in a stand of spruce, waiting for deer. When they saw the wolves enter the glade they opened fire on them. The wolves were over three hundred yards away, far enough for them to escape. But the death noise came again, repeated many times and one of the subordinate wolves fell dead as they scurried back into the safety of the underbrush.

The men's gunfire was followed by human noises and shouts at the sight of the fallen wolf. Midnight led the wolves away from the scene of death. They did not return for many weeks. By then the fallen wolf's carcass had been eaten by ravens and other predators. His pelt had been taken and all that remained were parts of the skeleton. The wolves had never seen this before. They were confused. What kind of hunter would take only the pelt of an animal and leave behind the most important part, the carcass?

*   *   *

As the first snow hastened the coming winter and leaner days, Midnight led the wolves on daily hunting expeditions. By now, the pack would follow Midnight anywhere. He had completely won their confidence by his fearless attacks on large game, netting them more food than under Smoke's leadership. The pack had many successful kills and their storehouses were full early into the season. As the earth froze and the ice and snow came, these caches were safeguarded from rot.

The pack was on the trail of an old moose. He had seen them coming down the hill, their dark shapes revealed in the moonlight, gliding over the ice-crusted snow like shadows of death. He had survived many winters, had been through many fierce battles, had fought off ravaging attacks of wolf packs and had survived. He had been gored by the antlers of a bull moose in a struggle that had left a terrible jagged scar on his chest where the fur would no longer grow.

The wolves had lived through another winter but were inevitably hungry once more. They would not give up their hunt now that they had his scent. They would be coming after him with relentless determination.

But this old warrior would not run. He would die fighting for his life. He would maim and gore as many wolves as he could before he gave up his flesh to them. Sometimes, when an animal battled too ferociously, a wolf pack would leave him alone.

But he sensed that would not be the case this time. The pack was coming after him at a rapid pace. When the snow was softer and deeper he could elude them, outrun them with his long legs. But they were running hard on top of the ice-covered snow. The wolves' weight did not break through this surface and they were running on the brittle crust, making fairly good time and closing the gap quickly.

*   *   *

Midnight and the pack were eager for the kill. They had been steadily hunting for weeks and had encountered only small game. They had stopped at one of their winter storehouses and quickly devoured all the contents.

Midnight was the first to pick up the scent of the moose as he wandered through their territory. The large animal was moving upwind from the pack, over a mile away. But there was something familiar about this scent to Midnight. It was more than just the smell of any moose. He had come across this particular scent before. It lingered in his memory, urging him on.

The pack was hungry and tensed to battle the large animal. Their strength was in numbers. Alone, one wolf would not try to take down the moose, but with the combined strength of the pack the animal would tire. If the moose ran, their task would be less hazardous. Running, he became easier prey for them. They would hack away at him from all sides until he collapsed from exhaustion.

Midnight led the wolves over a ridge. The pack followed so closely behind Midnight that they had no time to react to the icy surface on which they suddenly found themselves. Ahead was a long, sloping hill with a steep incline. The surface was slick and smooth. There was little foliage or trees and hardly a bump to give them purchase. The wolves lost their footing and skittered wildly down the slope, sliding in a long, frantic descent to the bottom. They crashed into the drifts of snow below, cracking the layer of ice and landing in an explosion of white powder. Unable to gain control in the soft, exposed snow, the wolves who brought up the rear collided with the wolves below them.

Only Moon, who had approached the crest of the hill tentatively, stood at the top and watched the comic activities of the pack. When they had all reached the bottom and were busy disengaging themselves from one another she stepped over the edge on all fours and slid down the hill after them. She made a complete circle and landed in the soft snow near Midnight. The pack recovered from their romp and shook the snow from their bodies.

Farther up the valley, sheltered in a stand of pine, the old bull moose watched and waited. The pack would be coming for him soon. He was upwind from them and they would still have his scent. There was no way he could avoid them. Whatever he elected to do, they would soon be on him. He dug in and waited for the death struggle that was inevitable.

*   *   *

The old moose weighed almost three quarters of a ton. His antlers spread fully six feet across and each contained a dozen tines. Soon he would lose both antlers as spring approached but now they were still formidable weapons. His bell, a large growth of skin that hung under his chin, swayed as he moved his huge head. The long deep scar on his chest was mute testimony to his will and ability to fight.

His mate and two offspring were just north of where he stood. They had gone into the dense woods, seeking food and refuge from the wind and snow-laden fields. He stood at the edge of the forest and watched the wolves close the distance over the white floor of the valley. In the clear, crisp air the full moon lit up the night, its light laying a sparkling blue veil on the frozen landscape.

The wolves were coming fast. In the lead was the largest black wolf the moose had ever seen. Directly behind him trailed a pure white wolf, not nearly as big as the alpha, and behind her came the rest of the wolf pack. Overhead, a flock of ravens circled the pack. They would pick the old moose's bones clean if he lost the encounter with the wolves.

* * *

Midnight saw the huge bull moose in the light of the brilliant moon. He recognized the scent now and he connected the sight of the animal with the familiar smell. It was the same moose he had tracked last winter and had not fought. At that time Midnight was not wise enough to have won the battle. The moose was willing to fight then and was ready now. He stood his ground and watched Midnight and the pack come to him. He showed no sign of running.

Midnight pressed on, keeping the quick pace as he climbed the hill leading to the prey. Midnight would charge the bull moose head on and the pack would follow instinctively. It was dangerous to attack large animals head to head, but, if he was able to secure a powerful grip on a prey's muzzle, he could force the head to the ground. In this awkward position, if only for a few seconds, game was vulnerable. It was then that the pack would strike at the animal's flanks, underbelly and throat.

This time though, the pack slowed behind Midnight as they drew near the large bull moose. Midnight would consider his plan of attack a moment longer before he plunged into battle. The pack spread into a neat semi-circle around the gigantic beast, stalking him and waiting for a move by their leader. Midnight surveyed the animal who lifted his massive head, snorted and waved his antlers in defiance of the wolves. Then, he lowered his head and aimed his antlers at Midnight.

In a lightning swift motion, Midnight charged. He came across the hard snow directly into the moose's line of vision just as his head came up. Midnight's enormous canine teeth clamped on the moose's muzzle and drove deep into the flesh. The powerful jaws of the big wolf exerted tremendous pressure and shattered bone in the huge animal's jaw. In a fury, the great moose swung his head up, his overwhelming strength lifting Midnight clear off the ground. But the black wolf held on. The moose tried to dig at his tormentor with his antlers but Midnight kept his jaws clenched tightly over the moose's nose and mouth. Even though he was swung wildly in the air, he stayed out of reach of the killing antlers.

The great moose could not breathe and he was becoming desperate. The wolf's teeth had shattered his nostrils and he kept the moose's mouth jammed shut. The moose tossed his head ferociously from side to side, hoping to dislodge his attacker. The other wolves had moved to help their leader and were leaping at the big animal's flanks. He had been seriously bitten already and was beginning to lose blood.

Never before had the moose encountered so fierce a wolf pack, led by so daring an alpha male. He lifted his head high, bringing the large wolf up with the effort. Then he brought his head down swiftly, slamming the wolf into the frozen, bloodstained snow. Pain tore through his face as the weight of the wolf and the force of the impact ripped away part of his flesh. Still the wolf held on. From all sides the pack was hacking at him. He received a slashing cut across the belly that left fresh blood in the snow. He was quickly weakening.

Again, he brought up his great head, carrying the black wolf in a wild, sweeping arc. Down he came, furiously smacking the wolf to the turf. This time it worked. Midnight lost his breath and he was torn free. But the wolf's jaws never opened completely and, as he was broken free of the hold, he tore away part of the moose's face.

Now the great moose was free to fight. He would not make the mistake again of allowing the black wolf to get such a deadly grip on him. He swung his sharp antlers at the attacking wolves, slashing at them from both sides. He caught one gray wolf on the first thrust and sent him tumbling end over end in the snow, a bloody hole appearing in his side, where broken ribs protruded through the gored flesh. The wolf limped off, hurt and finished with the fight.

Just as quickly, the old moose caught another attacking wolf in front of him with a savage whack of his antlers, immediately breaking the animal's neck.

Midnight recovered from the crash to the snow-packed ground, sucking great gulps of air into his tortured lungs. He stepped out of range of the great beast's antlers and watched for a few moments as the moose gained momentum and began to rip the pack apart. If they were to kill this animal, the wolves were going to pay a heavy price with their own flesh and blood. He was a stubborn adversary who would not easily give up his life. When Midnight had fully recovered, he joined the pack in attacking the moose from the flanks.

During the time Midnight was engaging the moose some of the wolves managed to make telling wounds on the great beast. One male had scored a tremendous gash in the animal's vulnerable underbelly. The animal was losing a lot of blood. Other wolves had ripped at the old bull's haunches and were also opening wounds.

With this kind of constant harassment, it would not be long before the moose succumbed to the attack. His attackers would not relent. But still he fought courageously, not giving ground. Midnight moved cautiously around the moose, seeking an opening. The great beast gave him none. While fending off the attackers he kept a wary eye on the black wolf who was now circling him.

Midnight joined his male offspring on the moose's left flank. They stalked the old moose, seeking that one instant when they could get an opening and bring the moose to the ground. Already two lay on the snow, either dead or dying. Moon had been in the thick of it along with her offspring, but now she, like Midnight, followed his lead and stalked their prey.

The moose finally gave Midnight the opening he sought. One of the subordinate wolves tried to attack the moose from the front as Midnight had. The moose parried with his antlers, driving the wolf back. Still the wolf foolishly insisted on finding an opening. The sight and smell of the blood from the moose's wounds stirred him on. On his second attempt, the moose drove forward, his head lowered, as the wolf charged to meet him. The antlers collided with the wolf's chest, breaking bone and flesh, crashing the animal to the snow. The moose dug his antlers under the fallen wolf and, using them like a scoop, lifted the dead wolf high over his head. In the instant his head was held high, his throat presented the target Midnight wanted. He moved in a flash, his huge canines bared fiercely, and he struck a direct hit on the moose's exposed throat.

With one savage bite, he ripped the soft flesh wide open. Midnight held fast to the moose's neck, his jaws locked around the ragged flesh. With his weight moving downward, he drew the moose's head and antlers into the ground. His male offspring struck then and opened the belly wound even more. It was too much for the moose. He could no longer raise his head. He could not shake off the second attack by the huge black wolf. His eyes rolled backward and he collapsed in the snow.

The pack was on him in an instant, ripping and devouring flesh even before the animal died. Midnight released his hold and joined the others in gorging themselves. They would have plenty more food for their storehouses.

The pack had lost three subordinate animals in the battle. But the loss of lives was expected in the pack. The battle with the great moose had been the most ferocious fight Midnight had incurred since his reign as leader of the pack. He came away from the fight bruised and sore.

After the wolves had eaten the flesh of the fallen moose, they ripped off sections of meat and buried them in a large hole near the area where the battle had taken place. When they had stored all the food they wanted, they covered the hole with snow and ice and scent-marked the spot.

Once the pack had finished with the carcass of the dead moose, they left it for the flock of ravens who waited patiently, perched on pines at the edge of the forest. The large black birds descended on the remains and fed once again at the invitation of their friends, the wolves.

CHAPTER 9

M iles Coffin arrived at his house once again after many
frustrating months of running down blind leads tracking the black wolf. He had been trekking through the wilds of the
Alaska interior on his unending pursuit for almost a year and had
drawn a blank every time.

Coffin was on Midnight's trail within days of burying Lucy.
He knew the wolf had headed north. Given the distance the wolf
could travel in the snow Coffin calculated Midnight could have
been no more than a constant hundred miles or so ahead of him
during the time that he pursued him. But he knew also that the
wolf could have changed direction at any time. Coffin had lost
him somewhere along the way and had to rely on people inform-
ing him of possible sightings of the wolf.

He had printed descriptions of the wolf and mailed hundreds
of copies to every hunting lodge, inn, bar, organization or individual involved in hunting. Information drifted in over the months.
He followed up data that seemed solid. But with no luck.

It was late winter now. When Coffin arrived snow was piled
high around the cabin and ice hung from the roof. He got a shovel
from the shed and dug his way to the front door. The house was

cold. He threw some logs in the fireplace and quickly got a fire going. He skimmed through the mail that had collected. Most of it was junk but there were a few letters from people who thought they might have seen Midnight on hunts. Coffin didn't put much credence in them. None seemed certain. He couldn't follow every lead he received. He had to be certain before he ventured on a trip based on supposed sightings. It took time and money for each hunt he undertook. Coffin had enough money to last a few years, but he could not continue indefinitely.

He poured himself a drink and walked through the compound to the fenced pen. He left it exactly as it was when Lucy was killed by the wolves. Inside, he stood where she had died.

He wondered if there was anything he might have done to have changed the course of Lucy's terrible death? He answered himself. Yes. To begin with, he should never have kept wolves on the property once he brought Lucy into his world. He should not have placed her in such an environment when he knew the danger. He had handled the wolves himself but Lucy was not prepared. If she had only taken the precaution of bringing the gun into the pen with her. Killing one or two of the wolves at that moment could have bought her the precious time she needed to get out of the area.

He went back to the house with his own guilt reinforced. Once Midnight was dead by his hand, he swore to return here, tear down the pen and sell the place. Leave Alaska, start anew, try to forget. Forget Lucy. How could he forget Lucy?

There were many messages on the phone answering machine. He clicked it on and listened while he finished his drink. Most of the messages were not important to him, but one caught his attention. He rewound and played it back.

"Miles, this is Jim Fuller. Up north of Fort Yukon. I think we spotted your black wolf. Big one. Pure black. Patch of white on the chest. Give me a call . . ."

Coffin knew Jim Fuller. He had taken hunters out on more than a dozen trips from Fuller's lodge. Fuller was an experienced hunter and Coffin trusted his judgment. He dialed the number Fuller had left. Fuller was not there and Coffin had to leave a message. It wasn't until later in the evening that he got a return call.

"It's Jim Fuller, Miles."

"I got your message, Jim. You spotted the wolf? How sure are you?"

"I couldn't swear to it, but he sure as hell fits the description. Hundred forty or so pounds. Big wolf. All black. White chest."

"Is the white fur in a diamond shape?" Coffin asked.

"Yes. It looked diamond shaped, but it's difficult to tell from a distance. There aren't many wolves that fit that description. In fact, this is the first wolf I've seen who does fit it. I've spotted black wolves before, but none that big with the white fur in the right place."

"All right," Coffin said, excitement in his voice. "I'll be up in a few days."

"Listen, Miles. The wolf is running with a pack. I know you said he was a loner, but, if it is him, is it possible that he would join a pack?"

"Sure," Coffin replied. "Midnight is an aggressive, resourceful wolf. No reason why he couldn't fit in with a pack."

"But he was leading this one."

"It'd be just like Midnight to have taken over. He probably drove off the alpha male."

"If you're interested, Miles, and you plan on coming up here anyhow, would you consider making some fast money as a guide on a hunt?"

"Hunting what?" Coffin asked.

"Of all things, would you believe wolves?"

"Really? Wolves? I don't know if I can give you the time. How long?"

"Twelve days."

"I won't stay for twelve days. I've got to keep moving to find the wolf. He's not going to wait for me."

"The thing of it is, Miles, I could really use you on this one.

Your expertise. We're going to the territory where we saw your black wolf. We're going to hunt the pack he was running with."

"Who are the hunters you're taking?" Coffin asked.

"Group of businessmen from New York City," Fuller said. "Father and two sons. He's chairman of the board of a cosmetics company. Taylor Cosmetics. Maybe you've heard of it."

"Vaguely," Coffin said. "A cosmetics company. What the hell kind of hunters are these guys? I don't want to drag along a bunch of amateurs."

"No, not amateurs. They've been around. Big time. But they have never hunted wolves. The way I get it, they have plenty of trophies and want to add a wolf or two to their collection. They're willing to spend as much money as it takes."

"I'll tell you, Jim," Coffin said. "I'm not really interested in helping a few New York suits run down Midnight. I want him for myself. You know why. He killed Lucy. And I damn sure don't want him ending up as a trophy in some executive's home. No, he's got to die by my hand."

"Look, Miles," Fuller said. "We can help each other. I don't know if I can handle this without you along. It's just me and my partner, Willie Mason, here. We'll be using snowmobiles to hunt the pack and we need that third guide. We'll be tracking your black wolf and we'll make sure you get him."

"You don't really need me, Jim," Coffin said. "You and Willie can handle this."

"You are the third man. We'd rather have you. He's your wolf, Miles. We're going after the pack he's with and if you're not with us I can't guarantee that we won't get him before you do."

Coffin was silent for a few moments. "When is this hunt?" he said.

"In three weeks."

"I can't wait that long," Coffin said. "I could come up now and hunt him myself. You know that. Now that I know where Midnight is I want to go after him immediately."

"Hell, what have you got to lose by waiting a few weeks?" Fuller said. "The wolf will still be there."

"Tell you what," Coffin said. "I'll do it your way on one condition."

"Name it," Fuller said.

"Midnight is my kill and no one else's."

"You've got a deal, Miles."

* * *

One of the envelopes Coffin got in the mail was a letter from an insurance company notifying him that Lucy's life insurance policy had left him twenty five thousand dollars. They had been trying to contact him for months. He was to sign papers at an agency in Fairbanks. The letter was a jolt to Coffin, reminding him once again of the reality of Lucy's death.

He drove to Fairbanks, collected the money and deposited it to his checking account. He knew he would spend every penny in his effort to catch Midnight. Damn, he cursed. Money from Lucy's death. Dead and gone, forever. Never to be with her again. Never to be with her.

CHAPTER 10

The days slowly drifted by. Soon Miles Coffin would be on Midnight's trail once more. What would it be like having to deal with businessmen from a large city like New York? He could only imagine the type of hunter with whom he would be involved. Were they arrogant, viewing all animal life as only something to be trifled with for their own personal self-gratification?

Coffin was drinking more now that he was not out in the wild. At home despair was more prevalent than in the wilderness, where survival dominated every waking minute. Here, with nothing but time on his hands, Coffin drifted to the bottle to offset the effects of despair.

He tried once more to face Lucy's death by going into the fenced pen.

The gate had begun to rust. It squeaked loudly when he forced it open. There was no evidence of her death other than what existed in his memory. Where the wolves had died there was nothing left of their carcasses but bones that had been picked clean by insects and ravens. There was no loyalty when hunger was involved. Even the ravens, friends of the wolves, saw their bodies only as food.

Coffin spent a few days digging holes in the ground and buried what remained of the wolves he had killed. The activity helped him forget his misery and the liquor. For the time being.

Since he had destroyed his television set he had no idea what was happening in the world. The newspaper mail delivery was terminated since he had not paid the bill. All he had to rely on was radio. And even then he was inclined not to turn it on. He was allowing his own thoughts to become his universe. And he knew this was the quickest path to self destruction.

Buried within himself, he was brought out of the abyss of hopelessness by a sharp rapping at the front door.

He swung the door open and was faced by a man in full uniform. It was a game warden. Ted Neff. He knew him well from his days with the Game and Fish Department.

"Hello, Coffin," Neff said.

"Neff. What the hell are you doing out this way?"

"Can I come in? I'd like to talk to you."

"Sure. Come on in," Coffin waved Neff in. He took off his hat and nervously rolled it in his hands.

"Can I get you something?" Coffin asked. "A drink?"

"Coffee will do."

"I'll make some." Coffin threw on a pot, and found that he was down to very little in the can. It made him face reality. He needed to replenish much of his supplies.

"What can I do for you, Neff?" Coffin asked as he brought a full cup and set it down before the warden.

"This isn't easy for me, Coffin. We've known each other a long time. I want you to realize it's the job and it's nothing personal."

Coffin said nothing.

"It's like this. We know what you've been doing."

Coffin remained silent. He let Neff do the talking.

"Look, Coffin, you've been killing wolves. Quite a few. We understand the cause of your rampage and we sympathize with your loss. But you can't slaughter wolves the way you've been. You've got to call a halt to it."

Still Coffin did not speak.

"We think you've killed close to forty wolves in the last year. You've left a trail clear across Units 20 and 25. We've found carcasses along the Yukon River, by the Tanana, as far north as Chandalar Lake. We're sure it's you and not some hunters because you never bothered to skin the wolves. You're just blowing them away. You've been killing them from your plane even though you tried to cover what you did. We're on your case and you're bound to be caught."

"Did they send you all the way out here to tell me that?" Coffin finally said.

"Come on, Coffin. You know damn well you can't keep this up. What do you think you're doing?"

"Get the hell out, Neff," Coffin swore.

"That attitude won't help, Coffin. The Department is going to come down on you damn hard. You can wind up in jail, lose your plane."

Coffin merely stared at the game warden.

"But you know all that, don't you?" Neff said.

"Are you here to arrest me?"

"Not yet. I'm here to warn you. You're wrong. What you're doing is wrong. And you know it. Once we prove it, we'll move on you."

"Is that all?"

"Am I wasting my time coming here, Coffin? I didn't have to, you know."

"You're not wasting your time, Neff. As you said, you're just doing your job."

"What's the purpose of this slaughter?" Neff asked. "Do you intend to kill all the wolves in North America? When does all this end?"

"It ends when it ends."

PART TWO

CHAPTER 11

The painting was a failure and Andy Foster knew it. He had lost the elusive quality of sincerity he had been trying so hard to achieve. He dropped his palette and brush roughly on a paint-smeared tabaret and stepped back from the large canvas to see his work more objectively.

It was no use, he decided. The initial effect he had tried to capture had escaped him. What he envisioned the painting to be and what it was becoming were different. He blamed his failure on a recent lack of commitment. His subject, a construction worker perched on a girder high over the streets of New York City, lacked the emotion he had infused into earlier paintings. Technically, it was dazzling. The man was standing on a steel beam, alone, contrasted in shadow against the brilliant setting of the city below him. The background was done in toned-down, misty cool colors. The foreground, in warm colors, was dazzling against the multitudinous detail of the city streets. But there was something missing. Soul? Was that it? Had he left his own soul out of his subject matter? It needed to be revealed in the eyes of the subject; yet it wasn't there.

He felt the sudden urge to end the demands he had set for

himself in recent months. His goal was to complete a series of large oil paintings about the struggle of the working man in America. So far, he had successfully completed five canvases; a farmer plowing a field at sunrise, a fisherman hauling a catch in the rain, a steelworker in a fiery mill, an assembly worker in an auto plant and a fireman battling a blazing tenement. He planned to continue the series with as many more, but he was losing the enthusiasm he felt when he started.

The five completed canvases surrounded him, stretched out against the brick walls of the New York City loft in which he lived. They brought a dazzling burst of color into the monotony of his dreary quarters.

The paintings were good, he assured himself. They possessed the quality that had eluded him in his latest attempt. He had been inspired while creating them. He turned his back on the painting and walked to the other end of the loft where the work area was separated from the bath and kitchen. There had been only a sink and a badly stained toilet when he moved in. It had taken a good deal of effort and much of his meager income to get the loft into livable condition. He had painted the bare brick walls a stark white to aid the lighting. It helped. But white did not hold up long in the New York City environment. Within a few years the color was already a pale gray. The bathroom was the only truly separate room. Andy had a plumber rip out the old bowl and replace it and added a shower and new fixtures. The kitchen was a simple, efficient area with only a stove, sink and a small refrigerator. The remaining room was nothing more than a bare studio with a few chairs, a couch that converted into a bed and lots of artist paraphernalia.

Andy felt self-sufficient in his studio-home. He had what he needed to work and live. Except that money did not come easily from his paintings. His work so far had sold sparingly. He painted mostly large, realistic canvases which consumed a lot of time. In order to get a fair return for his labor and the materials he used he had to get a decent selling price. But people were reluctant to pay thousands for the work of an unknown artist. He had sold a few in the last year but those sales did not produce enough money to serve as an income.

Thank God, he thought, for his father, Maxwell Taylor, who granted him a monthly allowance to pay the rent. That money, every month, guaranteed the rent was paid. Everything else, art supplies, food, the necessities of life in Manhattan, had to be paid for from his earnings. In order to cover those costs Andy worked at low-paying jobs, precious time away from the canvases he had to finish. He served stints as dishwasher, busboy, factory worker; whatever paid the bills.

The gallery owner who handled Andy's paintings saw potential in his work and had talked him into producing more of the things that had sold. One large oil netted him over four thousand dollars. The painting was a stark, dramatic view of longshoremen unloading cargo on a New York dock with a grim winter view of the city behind them. Andy thought this sale might have established him as a bankable artist but he was soon to learn that the sale of one painting does not make a reputation. The gallery owner convinced him that paintings of this size and subject was the direction to pursue and insisted he deliver more. She wanted as many large canvases as he could produce for an upcoming show.

Andy was twenty-seven years old. He had the luxury of time on his side and another few years of toil might change his life completely if he continued to produce work that sold. Often, in times of mild despair, he considered the simple solution to his financial problems that had been held out to him. He had merely to pick up the phone and agree to accept an offer from Max Taylor that had been standing for years. He reflected on his father. Max Taylor was the head of a large cosmetics firm. Max had often tried to convince Andy to join the ranks of Taylor Cosmetics as a minor executive.

Andy's mother had been Max Taylor's mistress. Because she would not give up her baby to the entrepreneur, Taylor agreed to financially care for her and the child. He bought her a house on

Long Island and provided her with a modest lifetime income. Andy's mother never married and went to her grave still loving a man who gave only his money as evidence of his feelings for her.

Andy had seen Max Taylor only a few times since the day his mother had been buried over three years ago. Max had been standing outside the ring of mourners when she had been placed in the ground, his face pale and drawn. He was obviously saddened by her death. Afterwards, Andy walked beside the aging man.

"I loved her, you know," Max Taylor said simply.

It hadn't been easy turning Max down. Andy was promised a position as a vice-president alongside his older half-brother, Giff. Andy would start high up the ladder rather than at the bottom because Max wanted instant status for his sons. He believed that a person could learn the business from the top down just as well as from the bottom up. But Andy wanted no part of the offer. He graciously declined. He had dropped out of college to paint even though Max had been paying his tuition.

Andy was interested in art since childhood. Max Taylor knew this and tolerated that interest. But he had never taken Andy's talent seriously. Painting pictures was not business. It did not pay the bills. In Max's mind it was a foregone conclusion that Andy would join the firm when he came of age.

Andy believed Max would honor his commitment to art. He never realized Max had been patronizing him all along. Max believed a few years of suffering would bring Andy into the fold damn quick.

The relationship between Andy and his father had never been strained though. Andy loved Max Taylor and he knew Max returned that love in his limited manner. Throughout his lifetime his father played a serious, if not constant, role in his growth. There had never been any mystery in Andy's life about his father's identity. From early childhood the boy understood that Max Taylor was his father even though he was never to be considered a permanent part of the Taylor family.

The sudden sharp ring of the telephone shattered his thoughts. The familiar voice of his half-brother, Giff Taylor, spoke to him.

"Andy, how are you? It's Giff."

"Fine, Giff. I'm fine." Andy was truly surprised that Giff had called him. As far back in his memory as he could recall Giff had rarely initiated contact with the bastard son of the Taylor patriarch. "What's the occasion?"

"Does there have to be an occasion?"

"Don't shit me, Giff. This is Andy. Remember?"

For an instant Andy wondered if Giff was going to hang up. He had caught his half-brother off guard with his abruptness. But Giff was always domineering and Andy had learned to fend him off with strong verbal thrusts. Memories of early childhood rivalries lingered in Andy's mind. The boys had never gotten along well. Giff treated Andy as an interloper even though their mutual father regarded his sons as equals.

"Tell you why I called," Giff said, regaining his composure. "I want to get together with you tonight."

"What do you mean?"

"Meet somewhere. Have some dinner, drinks. Talk."

"This is kind of sudden, isn't it?"

"Well, I've been meaning to call you for a while, kid. But I've been so damn busy. You know how the corporation is."

"How's Max?" Andy asked.

"Max is okay. Getting older. Working hard. He never lets up."

"I haven't seen him for a while."

"That's partly why I want to get together with you," Giff said. "We got something big coming up that Max wants you included in."

"You're not planning to get little brother drunk and sentimental, are you? You know I don't plan to be an executive."

"Hell no, Andy. I leave that stuff to the old man. You like what you're doing, that's fine with me. I have nothing to say about what you do with your life."

"Is Max coming tonight?"

"No. Just you and me."

"All right," Andy said. "Where do we meet?"

Giff gave him the name and address of an uptown restaurant. "Just a night of drinks, food and bullshit," Giff added.

* * *

"You are the worst bastard that ever lived, Giff!" the young girl screeched.

Giff Taylor paused in the open door, his hand perched on the knob, and looked back at the person who had just cursed him. He smiled, cynically.

"I never pretended to be anything I wasn't," he said.

The girl began to cry softly. She was kneeling on the living room floor of her small apartment, both hands clutching her throat. She looked pitiful. For an instant he felt a slight pang of sympathy. He almost stepped back into the apartment but quickly thought better of it.

"Take care, Jenny," he said coldly, closing the door behind him.

"Bastard!" she cried. "You'll get yours! Someday, you'll get yours!"

It was raining and the streets of the East Village, where the girl's apartment was located, were riddled by the downpour. It took him almost fifteen minutes to flag a cab. The rain and the New York morning rush hour made it difficult to find one. He told the driver to head uptown and settled back in the rear seat. He wiped the drops of rain from his face and brushed back his thick brown hair with his fingers. The cold rain dropped down his neck like needles of ice. It was one of those raw mornings in New York when the temperature was hovering just above the freezing mark.

Giff reached into his shirt pocket for a cigarette. He lit it, disregarding the "No Smoking" sign mounted on the partition between him and the driver. He rolled the window down and let a trail of smoke out through his nostrils. It was instantly sucked out into the cold air. The chill felt good, Giff thought. It helped clear the cobwebs from his head.

He was going to miss Jenny, he thought. There hadn't been many women in his life quite like her. She knew how to satisfy a man. Their relationship had lasted a little over a year and Giff had spent more time and money with her than any woman before in his thirty-five years of life. He liked her enough to make it a steady thing between them. He picked up the rent on her apartment and had bought her a bright red sports car, a gift to certify their romance.

And yet he called an end to their affair. Abruptly, without explanation. He felt he was being smothered by her. It was the same pattern with her as it had been with other women in his past. They wanted to break his free spirit. Marriage, house in the suburbs, country club, kids; these were the last things on his mind. Settle down. Never. He did not want marriage and he was not about to be intimidated, no matter what he felt for her. He was a free man, young, good-looking, sitting on top of the world. Hell, his father didn't get married until he had made his first million.

Giff thought of his father today, at the age of seventy-five, as the epitome of the American male, successful, head of an international firm. Self-taught, he built the business from a shoestring operation he had started when he was in his early twenties. It hadn't been an easy road for the old man, Giff knew. But he was a sly fox and had always been a slave to his convictions. He believed that the American woman was very pampered and that she would someday make him enormously wealthy. He was right.

In those early days it didn't make sense for Maxwell Taylor to have been married. He had no time for a family and he was conning every woman buyer in every department store across the country he could into bed.

These days the old man didn't have to play that game with buyers anymore. The products sold so well that the buyers didn't matter. The women came to him . . . hell, Max was even into bed-

ding down the young models. Giff couldn't prove it; his father
kept his private life just that, private. But the old man spent a lot
of time with the ad agency. He had to be making it with the
young models who kept parading in when the agency cast the
commercials, Giff thought. Max was hardly ever home. He went
to the family mansion in Connecticut only for long weekends.
During the week Max spent most of his nights at his Manhattan
apartment. He claimed he was still a slave to work. Giff knew
better. The old man simply demanded control. Giff felt that if
Max retired he'd die. Giff had never heard him speak of stepping
aside and letting his son assume command. The idea was not part
of Max's thought process.

He couldn't imagine Max as dead. He'd have to picture him as
very old and frail. But the image wouldn't come. Max still drank a
goodly share of bourbon and finished a pack of Luckies every day.
Giff figured that when the senior Taylor died he'd go out like a
candle. No suffering. No lingering. Just finished. Hell, he might
live well into his eighties.

Giff wondered where he himself would be ten years from now.
Would he be in charge of Taylor Cosmetics, running the company
from Max Taylor's vantage point? Not if the old man hadn't retired
or died by then, he thought. And Giff felt he would have done
neither. Presently Giff served as president, but he did not run the
company. Max did. And Max would as long as he had life in him.

The cabbie stopped in front of the Taylor Building in mid-
town Manhattan. Giff tossed him a twenty-dollar bill as he got
out. It had stopped raining and the clouds were breaking up, revealing patches of blue sky over the towering thirty-eight floors of
the glass-and-steel structure.

Giff always felt a thrill of mild excitement when he saw the
building. It was a monument, he thought, a tribute to the man
who built it. It would stand as testimony to his resourcefulness
and determination. Maxwell Taylor had met the forces against him
head on and had won.

Now, Giff bore not only the fruits of the his forebear's efforts, but was relieved of the same pressures that drove that early pioneer to miraculous feats of achievement. The corporation's growth had created a new standard. It left Giff without worlds to conquer. And some day it would all be his.

There was a crowd of people marching on the sidewalk in front of the building. They were parading in a long circle before the entrance. Some held picket signs that protested the use of animals in testing cosmetics.

"STOP KILLING ANIMALS—OUTLAW THE DRAIZE TEST," one sign read.

"ANIMALS HAVE RIGHTS TOO," said another.

"THE DRAIZE TEST IS INHUMANE," quoted still another.

Giff pushed his way through the mob. There was a TV news crew setting up cameras. They were getting ready to interview some of the pickets.

The old man isn't going to like this, Giff thought, especially if it makes the evening news. The protesters decided to make an all-out attack against corporations who used animals to test their products and they were getting a lot of news coverage. This time it was Taylor Cosmetics' turn to receive the brunt of their attack. One TV news program had been showing films of the Draize Test, which Taylor Cosmetics and other companies used to test products for human consumption by using rabbits as guinea pigs. The rabbits were locked in stockades that held their heads in steady positions for the testers to apply chemicals to their eyes. These chemicals were used in the manufacture of products which women would eventually be wearing as eye makeup. When the rabbits showed signs of irritation around the eyes, the formulas were altered. The rabbits bore the brunt of experimentation that would make the products safe for distribution to humans. Many of the animals used in the experiments developed tumors around the eyes and went blind.

Giff entered the lobby without altercation. Luckily, most people did not know who he was. He boarded the elevator to his penthouse office. It was an express and was restricted for use only by the hierarchy of the company. The top three floors contained the executive offices which housed only the very-high-ranking corporate officials.

Giff's secretary, Mona Borden, an attractive, pert, middle-aged woman, met him as he stepped off the elevator.

"Your father's been calling for you," Mona greeted him.

"I figured as much," Giff answered.

"He sounds anxious."

"First, I'm getting into some dry clothes. And I need a shower and a shave. I'll call him when I finish."

"I hope he'll wait that long," Mona said.

"He'll wait."

Giff's office was at the northwest corner of the building facing Park Avenue. The outer walls were tinted glass from floor to ceiling and offered a magnificent view of the city. Mona's office was just outside his. There were only three other offices on the thirty-seventh floor, each on a corner and each occupying one quarter of the square footage of an entire floor. These were occupied by the executives directly answerable to Giff.

The thirty-eighth floor was inhabited by Giff's father, the CEO, Maxwell Taylor.

Adjoining Giff's office was a well-furnished, elegantly designed apartment. It contained a large living room, bedroom, kitchen, a lavish bathroom and a well-stocked bar. Giff entered the bathroom and quickly got out of his damp clothes. He ran the hot water in the sink and lathered his face with shaving cream. As he took the first stroke with the razor he considered himself in the wall mirror. No gray hairs. No receding hairline yet, he mused. But that would come. The old man's hair had receded back on his forehead and what hair was left was pure white. Giff still had the hard, trim body of his college days. He wouldn't allow himself to get soft. Although he smoked cigarettes he tried to compensate for his habit by working out regularly at a local gym. He even went a few rounds in the ring once in a while to prove he could handle himself. Anyhow, he assured himself, women loved a hard, lean body. He was not about to let his male attractiveness fade at a young age just because he was able to live well. Too many wealthy guys let themselves go to pot with too much rich food, booze and inactivity, he reflected.

As Giff finished shaving and turned to step into the shower he checked his reflection in the full-length mirror. There was a line of scratches on his back. Jenny. She got carried away during intercourse. Thinking about being coupled with her suddenly gave him an erection. He would miss her. He smiled as he stepped into the shower and soaped up. Yes, he was going to miss her. For a while anyhow. There were many others, just as good in bed, if not better.

When Giff came out of the bathroom his father was sitting in the living room waiting for him.

"Good morning," Giff said quietly. "I hear you were looking for me."

"You knew damn well I'd be looking for you," Max Taylor said. "Have you seen what's going on outside?"

"How could I miss it?" Giff said calmly as he selected a suit and fresh shirt from the wardrobe he kept in the apartment. He let the towel drop from his waist and slipped into clean underpants.

The elder Taylor saw the scratch marks on Giff's shoulder.

"Been getting much lately?" he asked his son in a subtle tone that implied an unspoken camaraderie.

Giff realized his father was referring to the marks that Jenny had made. He smiled slyly. "Enough," he said.

"She must have been a wild one," Max Taylor noted.

"Wild. Yeh, you could say that."

"Nothing serious?" Max Taylor questioned. Was that actually concern in his father's voice? Funny the old man should have suggested he might be serious about someone.

"Hell no," Giff answered. "God forbid."

Max grunted. Giff wasn't sure whether he was pleased or angry. It was hard to tell with him anymore.

"What are we going to do about these animal people?" Max Taylor asked.

"I don't know, Max," Giff said. The old man hated to be called anything but Max, even by his children. "What can we do? We'll just have to let this thing run its course. Just let the public relations people handle it. They're the experts in crisis management. We can't go down and bust heads."

"We could in the old days," Max commented, grunting again.

"This isn't the old days," Giff retorted. "I can't do much about them. They'll get on TV and people will rant and rave for about a week and then something else will get hot in the news and they'll forget all about us. Maybe just let it die."

"I'll bet half the women who are picketing on the street are using our products," Max snorted. "That's the fucking shame of it."

"They probably do," Giff said. "But they've got to have their cause. They rant about us using rabbits for experiments, claiming it's cruel. But they'll go home and eat a pork chop or a chicken without batting an eye or even thinking about the way animals are killed so they can feed their fat faces."

"It's not the same," the senior Taylor said. "They don't consider it cruel when the animal is used as food. They just look the other way. That's survival. What we're doing is not necessary. We're just pampering women. That's what we've been doing all along."

"I wonder how they would react to the idea that the collagen in our products, which millions of women use, is made from the remains of slaughtered animals and the afterbirth of humans."

"How do you think they'd react, Max? Another group would rise up against us."

"Maybe we can counter with an attack on women. They're the people who want the stuff we sell. We're only giving them what they want. The rabbits make it safe for them."

"We couldn't attack women, Max. We'd hurt our sales. Besides, these protesters are not all women."

Max crushed the cigarette he was smoking in an ashtray and stood up. "Most of them are," he said. "You're right, of course. We can't counter-attack women. I'm just pissed off."

"It'll blow over," Giff said. "Just let it die a natural death. These people will move on to something else; save the whale, save the trees. They'll be after the oil producers just to save Santa's reindeer. Who the hell knows?"

Giff watched Max pace nervously around the room while he finished dressing. He wants to know about Andy, he thought. That's really why he's here.

"I called the kid," Giff said, breaking the silence.

"And?"

"I'm going to see him tonight. We'll have dinner together. I'll ask him then."

"You haven't mentioned the trip yet?"

"No. I wanted to see him."

"Do you think he'll go with us?"

"I can't second guess him, Max. It's hard to say. He lives in his own strange world."

"This is important to me, Giff. I want him with us."

It rankled Giff to hear Max voice his devotion to his other son with seemingly sincere exigency.

"I hope you're not just wasting effort, Max. Andy never liked to hunt. You know that."

"I don't care if he doesn't want to kill anything," Max said. "I just want him along. He's not anti-hunting. He's been with us before."

"Sure. And the last time he showed us exactly how he feels. Got sick when he dropped that deer. He's caught up in that odd life he lives now. For all I know he resents me asking him to come. He thinks I want him in the company."

Max became sullen. "I should go to him myself."

Giff straightened his tie. He turned away from the mirror and smiled at Max.

"I'll see him tonight, Max. I'll lay it on the line. But I guarantee nothing. I can't force him."

* * *

Andy met Giff in a small French restaurant on the West Side in the theater district. Giff was sitting at the crowded bar, sipping scotch and puffing on a cigar when Andy entered. He raised his arm and signaled his presence to his younger brother.

The place was mobbed. It was just before curtain time. Andy joined Giff at the bar.

"What're you drinking?" Giff asked.

"A beer," Andy replied. He suddenly felt out of place in his sheepskin coat and jeans. He was surrounded by people in business suits and evening gowns. As he reached for his drink he realized there was paint pigment lodged under some of his fingernails.

"How's it going?" Giff asked, trying to sound nonchalant.

"It's a struggle, Giff."

"You'll make it, kid," Giff said flippantly. "I have faith in you."

Andy took a gulp of the beer. He didn't respond to Giff's remark. He knew Giff really did not have faith in him and regarded his endeavors as childish and a complete waste of time. Giff was not inclined to embrace the arts in any form. His world was, and had been for as long as Andy could remember, dominated by a narrow point of view restricted solely to personal gain and to sustaining the image he had of himself and his role in the business world.

Not that Giff was against the arts. He was not naive enough to negate their importance. Along with many of his business peers, he would willingly invest in a painting that he believed would grow in value, or throw some money into financing a show. The arts were nothing more than another business to him. It was the artist himself Giff treated with disdain; not his or her product.

"Hell, kid," Giff said. "When was the last time we got together?"

"I don't know. A year maybe."

"Selling any paintings?"

"A few."

"It's a hard world out there. Dog eat dog," Giff commented. "I guess."

"It doesn't get any easier, you know. Takes money."

"I'll be all right. I survive."

"It's all in your point of view," Giff said. "Some guys' survival is a lot better than others."

"Yeh," Andy said. "I've heard that."

"You've got to take it while you can," Giff expounded. "Whenever an opportunity presents itself you've got to grab it. How do you think Max built the company to what it is today? He jumped on the other guy and bought him out. Growth. Seizing the moment."

"I'm not exactly the predator type."

"Hell," Giff said, "we're all predators. Just like animals. They take whatever they can. They kill to live. Man is no different. He kills in a different way. He is a ravenous animal who lives off his fellow man. One guy preys on the other guy's weakness. Just like the beast in the forest who kills for food."

"You're probably right," Andy agreed.

"I know I'm right," Giff said.

When they sat down to eat and the waiter stood by the table, Andy leaned over to Giff and said quietly, "I don't have much money, Giff. So let's take it easy."

"This is on the company, kid. I invited you, remember. Besides, you're Max's son. What the hell are you worrying about money for?"

"Are we back to that again?" Andy said. "Is that really the purpose of tonight?"

"Look, Andy," Giff said, obviously annoyed. "I'm not going to shit you. You know it's hurting Max that you won't come into the company. All right. That's your business. That's between you and Max. But that doesn't mean you can't take money from him that he's willing to give."

"I've taken money. I'm already in debt to him."

"Hell, you're not in debt to him. He doesn't expect anything in return from you. He's your father."

"He does expect me to join the company."

"No. You're wrong. He doesn't expect you to join. He wants you to join. There's a difference. How can you fault Max for that? He's wanted you to be with us all your life."

"I don't fault him, Giff. And I don't want him to be responsible for me."

"But you're his son, damn it! He can't change that. He feels responsible."

Andy recalled his mother saying almost the exact same words to him many times. As he had grown to maturity, and was introduced to his father's world, he became confused. As a child, he couldn't grasp the significance of the two worlds in which he lived. He was allowed to visit the Taylor estate, to play with his half-brother, to receive gifts from Max Taylor, to be supported by him, and yet his real life was only with his mother.

It wasn't until Andy was in his teens that the truth finally registered. Max Taylor was ashamed of having sired him. Some noble gesture had forced him to ensure that the boy and his mother were taken care of financially. But Max bore that responsibility from a distance. Although he projected the image of a loving benefactor, Max was never a true father to the boy.

"You know how I feel," Andy said. "I've got to paint. Can't Max just let it go?"

"Hell, kid," Giff said. "I told you I wasn't here to try and talk you into coming into the firm. I won't do Max's dirty work for him. It's up to him to personally speak to you about it."

Andy did not reply. Throughout his life he had been witness to his half-brother's wiles and deceptions. In Andy's opinion Giff was a narrow-minded man who would resort to whatever means possible to get what he wanted. He was shrewd and calculating and, backed by a battery of staff lawyers, used the law to his advantage. Against his business adversaries he had been a dangerous and volatile enemy. Andy had heard tales of Giff's ruthlessness in order to obtain his goals.

As a child, he had witnessed Giff's blatant and callous nature.

The memory that stuck in his mind of Giff was of a person not to be trusted.

"Listen," Giff said. "I'll level with you. There is something Max does want."

"What's that?"

"It's the main reason I'm here tonight. We're going on a hunt in about a month. Max wants you to come along. Like old times."

"A hunt." Andy was incredulous. "I can't believe it. Max wants me on a hunt with him. Hell, Giff, I haven't gone in years."

"I realize that. So what. What do you say?"

"Max asked that I go?"

"Damn right he did. The hunt was Max's idea. A reunion. It's a big deal for him. Means a lot."

"Damn," Andy said. "I wasn't prepared for this. Is it that important to him?"

"Very important, I'd say."

"I've got a lot of unfinished work," Andy said. "I'm trying to meet a deadline for a show. It will be my first. Do you know how important that is to an artist?" He knew as soon as he had spoken that Giff didn't care one way or the other.

"Work harder when you get back. It's just as damned hard for Max and me to break away. We'll only be gone for a couple of weeks."

"Right now I don't have that kind of time to spare."

"I'm not going to pressure you," Giff said. "The invitation stands. It would do great things for Max if you were there with us."

"What are you hunting?"

"Wolves," Giff said cheerfully.

"Wolves! Are you serious?" Andy was incredulous.

"Great idea, isn't it?" Giff was excited. "How many people can say they've actually hunted wolves?"

"I thought it was illegal."

"Not at all. As long as you follow the rules. We're heading deep into the Alaska interior. There are plenty of wolves still alive up there and legal to kill."

"Sounds pretty tough," Andy said. "Won't we have trouble running them down?"

"We hunt them on snowmobiles with shotguns. It couldn't be easier."

"You know my heart isn't in hunting," Andy said.

"Hell, you don't have to kill any. Just come along. Make the old man happy in his old age."

Andy finished eating. He pushed the empty plate away. He looked straight into Giff's eyes.

"Why wolves, Giff?" he asked.

"Why not wolves?" Giff replied cynically.

CHAPTER 12

M ax Taylor sat at the head of the huge, highly polished mahogany table in the center of the conference room in the executive offices of Taylor Cosmetics. Giff sat, as usual, at his right. Twelve other executive officers bordered them on both sides, their papers and notepads laid out before them. It was not a happy group. Their grim faces bore testimony to the fact that the meeting was not held to discuss good news.

Max had no paperwork in front of him (he prided himself on the fact that he never took notes) and his image was reflected clearly in the shiny top of the conference table. Max was a few inches under six feet tall, shorter than both his sons. Always slim and wiry, he gave the impression of being taller than he actually was. His receding hairline ended with a tuft of wispy white hair that streaked his skull like freshly fallen snow. When he stood up his image plunged deeper into the surface of the table.

"Now," Max said to the officers of the company, "I want these rabbit people out of here. And I don't give a damn how you do it."

There was a sudden rumble of comments amongst the men at the table as they turned to one another and voiced their thoughts.

"Let's have some ideas," Max said. "I've got my own way of

solving the problem. But I don't think it would pass approval at this table."

Giff grimaced slightly, thinking of Max organizing a goon squad to bust heads, the way he successfully kept the unions out of his company's plants when Giff was a little kid. He remembered his father's tirades when strikers had tried to shut down his New Jersey plant and had picketed to form a union. Max had cursed them for their audacity to make demands on him. From his point of view they ought to have been grateful they had jobs because of his efforts and the financial risks he had taken. When the strike lingered for a week he brought in strike breakers who plunged into the picket line and threw it into chaos. Miraculously, no one had been seriously hurt. But Max had his way. He had not been unionized.

The officers surrounding Max began to toss ideas at him. He dismissed many before their thoughts had been fully voiced. Some of the solutions amounted to appeasement and Max would have none of it.

"Look," he shouted. "I want to get rid of these people. Fast! And without giving in to any of their demands."

"We can't just force them to leave," one vice president interjected.

"Why the hell not?" Max asked.

"We have the image of Taylor Cosmetics to think of," the executive responded.

Max stared down at the man who spoke. He made it a point to tower over executives by standing at meetings. It intimidated them.

"Bull," he retorted, banging his fist on the table. "We are not a public company. We don't have thousands of shareholders to deal with. I am Taylor Cosmetics. And I don't want these fanatics attacking my company."

Max's comments about the lack of stockholders struck a sour note with Giff. The issue of selling the company stock in a public offering had been a controversial one between Giff and his father. Max would have no part of his son's proposals. Giff wanted Taylor

Cosmetics to become a public company and offer shares to a wide range of buyers. Giff would expand the company far beyond the level achieved by Max. A public offering would bring in a fresh supply of money that would finance the expansion he planned. And Giff's holdings would make him a richer man. Why wait till the old man dies?

"Then how can these humane people harm us?" the young executive asked. "We should just ignore them."

Giff had the feeling he would not be around the firm much longer if he continued to press Max like that.

Max looked directly into the outspoken executive's eyes. "Because, my young friend, they are bringing attention to us. They are camping on our front doorstep and they are pointing us out to the entire nation as ruthless bastards. The damned media picks this stuff up. They hate the corporate world and they must fill every minute of their airtime with something. They are the ruthless people. They pick out a company or an individual and make him a villain and the public eats it up. Then try to change that image."

The targeted executive fell silent.

"Max," one of the senior officers said, "Wouldn't it be a good idea to drop the tests on rabbits for a while? Just till things calm down."

"And give in to them," Max cried. "That's the absolute wrong thing to do. Then every damn group in the country with a trumped-up cause will find some reason to pick on us. Like hell I'll discontinue what we've been doing for years."

"I thought it might stop this national TV coverage if we stopped the tests," the senior executive said. "It would help our situation and we can halt some tests and announce to the press that we have."

"Damn it," Max retorted. "No. The bastards aren't going to tell me how to run my business. You join ranks with Giff here. He thinks these animal people will go away if we just turn our backs on them."

"Not exactly, Max," Giff countered. "I'm not saying we should do that at all. But I don't think we should confront them. Why give them what they want? The press loves to cover controversial issues. If we brace them they'll make more of it. Counter them by good public relations. The public will bore of them. Just give it a few more days. It will settle itself."

"Giff may be right," the senior executive said tentatively.

"And suppose they don't go away?" Max said. "I've seen some of these causes go on for years. They never give up. I don't intend to change company policy. And they won't give up their cause. These bastards could be out front every day for a long time."

"The press won't cover them all the time," Giff said. "They will move on to something else. It's their nature."

"Give it up, Giff," Max said bluntly. "Your idea stinks. We have to be forceful to stop them cold."

Giff didn't respond. He did not want to get into an argument with Max in front of the company executives. He knew his father well enough that challenging him, especially in front of his employees, would only provoke him. If Max was against something he would continue to be against it with all his might.

"How about if we force them into doing something stupid?" another executive offered.

"Like what?" Giff asked.

"If we can antagonize the pickets they might do something careless. Something against the law."

"Discredit them?" Max said. "Make them look bad?"

"Yes."

"Not bad," Max said, rubbing his hand on his chin, seemingly contemplating his next move. "There's an old trick," he said, "of infiltrating the picket line with some of our own people and have them start trouble. Have them throw rocks at the front of the building. Break a few windows. Wreck some cars. Start fires. That would turn the tide against the pickets."

"Hell, Max," Giff said. "We can't go around starting riots."

"Sure we can," Max replied. "That's the way to get results. It worked before. There's no reason it can't work again."

Giff wanted no part of Max's scheme to start trouble in front of their headquarters. But he had to act quickly. He had an idea kicking around in his mind but he hadn't put it into words.

"I want to try something," he said. "It'll have to be approved and done quickly. But I think it would be a proper balance to the negative image the pickets are painting of us."

"And what is that?" Max said, his voice ringing with indignation.

"I want to produce some print ads. Fast. Some TV commercials too. We can have our ad agency turn them out quickly and substitute them in slots for our regular commercials."

"What's the content?" Max asked.

"Positive thoughts," Giff replied. "We'll show the public all the good we've been involved in. Like the millions we've contributed to so many foundations. Cures for disease, save the environment. That sort of thing."

A murmur of approval ran around the room. The men at the table were smiling.

"I see you all seem to like Giff's idea," Max said.

There was a general nodding of heads.

"So do I," Max said. "Get it going."

*　*　*

"Is Andy going with us?" Max asked Giff later in his office.

Giff watched his father draw deeply on a cigarette and crush the stub out in a desk ashtray. He remembered when he was a child that his father blew smoke rings to entertain him. He had been fascinated to watch them come so perfectly from Max's mouth and spread into the air. He remembered also that Max always got the end of his non-filtered cigarette wet. Giff noticed that he still did.

"I don't know, Max," Giff answered. "It's damn hard to tell

with Andy. He would never listen to reason. He always went his own way."

"I'm aware of that. How did he react to the suggestion of the wolf hunt?"

"He seemed interested. He claims he has a lot of work to finish. He wouldn't commit himself to an answer. You know he has no love for hunting and he's so damned involved with his work."

"He's got to come. It may be the last trip we'll have." It disturbed Giff that Max sounded desperate.

"Look, Max," he said. "The kid respects you. He feels indebted to you. He won't go for my sake. You're going to have to talk to him."

"I thought it would be better coming from you," Max said. "I don't want him to feel pushed or obligated. You and Andy have to get along together for a long time after I'm gone. It's better if you start now."

"Hell, Max," Giff said, trying to sound cheerful, "you're going to be around for a long time. You'll probably outlive both of us."

*   *   *

"I'm sorry about your father, Giff," Mona Borden said to him as she fastened the last button on her blouse. She had just spent the evening with Giff at a hotel in Manhattan. In the few years she had worked for him, Giff had taken her to bed no more than half a dozen times. He had analyzed her properly as an opportunist. He knew she was an easy mark from the first time he worked with her. He brought her into his private life because her ten years with Taylor Cosmetics and her contacts in the company were invaluable.

Mona was married but that didn't seem to bother her. She was in her late thirties and was, Giff judged, not a bad lay. She had worked in the executive secretarial pool for six years before she moved up as a private secretary to some higher-ranking corporate officers. She acquired inside information which Giff needed and she was willing to sell. She got her data from the grapevine that wound its way through the fiber of the company. One personal secretary had lunch with another and rumors became fact.

Giff kept his finger on the pulse of the company by pretending he enjoyed Mona's company. He got bits of miscellaneous rumors from her which he fitted into the constantly changing structure of corporate life.

"What about my father?" he asked.

"The cancer. It must be difficult for you now."

Cancer. Max had cancer? It hit him with a jolt. Why didn't Max tell him? No. It would be just like Max not to let him know. His own son didn't know of his condition and yet secretaries in the company knew. He wondered if Max had told Andy. No, he wouldn't have told the kid either. Damn, he swore, what a fucking situation.

"Yes," Giff said, as if it were a burden he endured with the dignity of silence. "It's been tough."

"I'm so sorry," Mona repeated. "If there's anything I can do, all you have to do is ask."

"No. Nothing, thanks," he said, ending it.

As soon as the opportunity presented itself Giff got the details about Max's condition from his doctors. They insisted they were sworn to secrecy and he insisted that since Max was an old man and would die anyhow, the chances would be questionable whether Taylor Cosmetics would retain their services when he took over. He got what he wanted.

So the old man had cancer and was not given much time to live. Months, a year, maybe. So that's what the wolf hunt was all about. A last chance for him to be with his sons as a final reunion. A gesture to end his life the way he had lived it. And that's why he had insisted Andy come along. There would be no more chances for redemption.

Andy. Giff swore at the thought of his brother. Max's illegitimate son. He didn't belong. He never had. He was the product of a mistake. One mistake. Max and his mistress. One lousy mistake and someone who didn't belong becomes his brother. Giff thought about the future without Max. He knew he would take over the company operation. It was inevitable. No doubt about it. But where would Andy come into the picture? The estate and most of the stock Max held in the company would naturally go to Giff and his mother. But just how much would Andy inherit? Could he make trouble?

Damn the kid, Giff swore. Damn his hide.

*   *   *

Max Taylor couldn't tell anymore if the pain was getting worse. It wasn't sharp or crippling yet, as he expected it would be. It was, rather, a dull, gnawing discomfort he felt constantly, mostly suppressed by drugs. It would, he knew, get progressively worse until he wouldn't be able to bear it. By then the cancer would kill him as it spread.

His doctors pleaded with him to begin therapy. Many people, they claimed, had been saved by treatment. What was the percentage, Max had asked. No guarantees, he was told. Not good enough. Not what he called good betting odds. He would not grovel for his life, hoping some miracle cure would save him at the last minute.

He sat alone in his office, pondering his fate. He wasn't afraid of death, only the humiliation of an ignoble exit. He vowed he would not end life as a sobbing shell. Pride would not allow it. He swore he would snuff out his life by his own hand rather than slowly fade away in a hospital bed.

Time, he mused. How illusive it really was. Yesterday, a thousand yesterdays, were only minutes away. There was so little left with still so much to do. He wondered how he would stand up to the physical strain of the wolf hunt in less than a month. Even that one month could take a severe toll on his condition. He might not be able to keep the date.

Max still felt relatively strong. The effects of the cancer had not yet handicapped him but he wondered how much longer it would take before he could no longer function normally. The doctors had given him six months to a year. He resigned himself to the fact that his time had come and there wasn't a damn thing he could do about it. Just as well, he thought. Let the next generation earn their keep. It's time for them to take over. It was a new world anyhow. Not like when he started out. All he had were a few formulae for cologne while working in a tiny perfume factory on the Lower East Side of Manhattan. After a few difficult years selling to female buyers in many major department stores around the country Max decided to struggle for himself instead of selling for some indifferent employer.

He went into debt producing the packaged image which still decorated the millions of bottles, jars, tubes that sold to women around the world. They weren't aware that the cosmetics were manufactured in a little building in Brooklyn. In those days there did not exist the stricter government regulations of today. It was a hell of a lot easier to start a company from scratch back then. All a man really needed was fortitude, determination and a little capital. It was simple to define friends, enemies; easy to put problems behind you.

Nowadays, he felt, everything was stacked against building a company like his from the ground up. Today many firms faced new challenges. They were constantly taken to task for many apparent violations of environmental "ethics," chemical dumping, radioactive waste, polluting the atmosphere, ruining waterways, destroying plant life, maiming and killing animals unnecessarily. Max blamed much of the problems on one piece of modern technology that changed the way America and the world responded: instant communication, television.

It was virtually impossible to convince officials to look the other way. Some group was always riding herd on both government action and corporate activities. And they were always getting TV time. There had been so many exposures of corporate "greed" lately, both in the press and on television, that he actually had been braced to accept his turn. Would the world really be any better for all their efforts? He wondered.

At five o'clock he showered, shaved and put on a fresh suit. He thought of his rendezvous with his current mistress and became immediately aroused. He had many mistresses throughout his life, but she set off a sexual desire in him like few of the others.

When he got to the lobby of the Taylor Cosmetics building he saw that the picket line was still moving in a slow circle on the sidewalk. A news truck was parked in front of them and a crew had set up cameras and sound equipment. Max pushed through the pickets, cursing softly to himself in an effort to get to the street where his chauffeur-driven Rolls waited for him.

"It's him!" someone yelled. "Maxwell Taylor! The big shot!" Others began to block his way.

"It's Maxwell Taylor!" they shouted. "The head of the company."

Max suddenly found his path blocked. He was almost completely surrounded by pickets. A newsman appeared in front of him, brandishing a microphone. Behind him the inevitable camera crew moved in.

"Mr. Taylor," the newsman said, shoving the microphone forward until it was practically in Max's face. "Will you say a few words about animal testing? Do you intend to stop using animals?"

"No," Max said.

The commentator persisted. "Our viewers would like to know how Taylor Cosmetics intends to respond to the allegations of brutalizing rabbits in the Draize Test."

"Fuck you!" Max shot back.

"Cut that," the newsman said to his crew. He continued to pursue Max who was trying desperately to push past him.

"We are speaking to Maxwell Taylor, CEO of Taylor Cosmetics, about the disastrous effects on rabbits conducted by his company . . ."

"The hell you are," Max said, shoving the man who still blocked him.

"Mr. Taylor," he insisted, jamming the mike towards Max. "Does Taylor Cosmetics intend to end the brutality . . ."

"Get the hell out of my way!" Max shouted.

The man wouldn't move. Max had enough of it. His patience had been stretched too far. He threw a surprise punch up from his waist and his right fist caught the newsman on the point of his chin. It was a picture-perfect uppercut. The commentator's legs turned rubbery under him and he slumped to the sidewalk. The stunned crowd parted as Max pushed his way to the street.

Later, when he finally got to his mistress's apartment, he was doubly content. He saw himself punching out the newsman on the evening news and he overreacted to his spurt of physical violence with a show of sexual enthusiasm he was not aware he was still capable of.

∗   ∗   ∗

Max Taylor sat in the trophy room of his mansion, brooding. He had fallen into a period of deep melancholia which he could not shake. He left his office in New York early on Friday and came directly home to Connecticut. He was afraid his mood would slip into depression and might be obvious to everyone around him.

He had to be alone. He thought that a period of isolation and reflection would alter this chagrin. He wanted to die courageously. He did not want to be whipped like this, an admission that he had lost control of his destiny. He did not want to end his life pleading to a Maker he did not believe in.

The wolf hunt. The last chance to gallantly join his sons against an adversary that would stretch his endurance, a last chance to leave behind a memory of him as a vital force that would not give up. It would be cold in Alaska, even in early spring, but that would not be a deterrent. They had hunted caribou in the tundra of northern Canada, moose in Newfoundland, many others, all in similar weather. But they had never before hunted the wolf. It would be a great and novel experience for him as well as for his sons. For him it would be the last and maybe the best hunt of his life. For his sons it would be his last gift to them. When he suggested the hunt to Giff he was surprised how favorably his older son had reacted to the idea.

"Why the hell didn't I think of wolves?" Giff had said at the time. "That's fantastic. It's got to be one of the best ideas I've heard in years. Max, you're a genius."

Max didn't like the idea of pressuring Andy. There were other ways, he realized. He could have played upon his younger son's sympathy and announce to him that he was facing his end days. It would, therefore, be a great personal favor for the boy to agree to his father's wishes. But Max would not. As always, his pride stood in the way. Yet he had no time to wait. In the past, the camaraderie associated with a hunt had always drawn them into a tighter bond. It could work again.

Max remembered with fondness the celebration he had with his sons when they mounted the stuffed head of the bull moose Giff had shot. They had gathered in the trophy room at the Connecticut mansion and had happily gotten drunk together.

Giff's mother frowned on Max's drinking jaunts with his sons. She never interfered in Max's life, but she took exception with his drinking, particularly with Giff. Max knew she harbored no affection for Andy. The boy was the product of a long-standing adulterous relationship, a fact Max's wife lived with for many of the years of her marriage. Andy was brought into her household as the half-brother of her only son, acknowledgment that the boy was to be accepted as such.

The huge den was dark except for a low fire in the massive stone fireplace. The light from the flickering flames illuminated the mounted heads on the walls, making them appear alive. The dead eyes seemed to watch from stuffed craniums.

Max lifted his bourbon and held it out in front of him at arm's length. He saluted the bull moose mounted on the nearest wall.

"Here's to you, old moose," he said. "You were a good one."

The heads strung the walls in a span around Max, mute audience to his thoughts. He could contentedly live out his remaining days right here, he thought; die with the animals he had hunted during his life. A little poison in his drink and it would be all over. Except that his sons would know he had given up, that he had taken the easy, quick way out. He wanted to die without them knowing about the cancer. He wanted to die the way he had lived. With energy. With style. Quickly.

There was no way to reverse what is. His eyes roamed to the animal heads surrounding him. They rested on a rhino taken in Africa when Giff was a baby, before Andy was born. He had traveled a great distance for that one. There were deer, elk, caribou, a cougar taken in Montana. Most of the trophies had been his kills but there were a few contributions from Giff.

Throughout the years he and Giff had made at least two to three hunting trips every year. Sometimes only for a weekend, sometimes longer. Andy had been an infrequent guest. He finally shot a deer when he was almost twenty. It was the only animal he had ever killed. On the following hunts on which Andy had gone, Max recalled, he had never fared as well as he or Giff. He had aimed and fired but never hit anything. Andy was, at best, a reluctant participant who was with them only because of his father's urging.

Max was not naive. He knew Andy was not cut in the same mold as he and Giff. Andy was not a hunter. He did not like to bring down an animal.

"Why do you kill them?" Max remembered Andy's question when he had first brought the boy to the Connecticut house and he saw the mounted heads. He was around eight years old at the time and it was his first venture into his father's world.

Max tried to explain how he felt to the boy.

"It's the nature of the world, Andy," he said, knowing it was not easy to explain his thoughts about hunting to a boy whose world consisted of playing with a puppy in a small backyard and seeing animal life through the warped cartoons of television and movies. "Every creature that lives has to die. Even you and me. One animal is the food that others eat. Animals hunt other animals to live. Men are animals who also hunt animals to live, to eat."

The boy's eyes had widened in disbelief. "Did you eat all those animals on the walls?" he asked.

Max was sure he was not going to ever justify his position to Andy. He smiled. "It's a little more complicated than that, Andy. Some animals are hunters. Others are not. Man is the same. Some hunt, some don't."

"Am I going to be a hunter when I grow up?" Andy asked.

"I hope so, son. I would like that," Max had replied.

The den door opened, letting in a long stream of artificial light. His wife entered. She closed the door behind her, shutting out the sudden brightness. She came silently across the room and stood beside him.

"What's the trouble, Max?" she said softly. "Do you want to talk about it?"

Max turned to her, a faraway look in his eyes.

"I've given you a rough time of it over the years, haven't I?" he said, his voice faltering.

"I haven't complained."

"No. You never have. It must have been difficult for you."

She clutched his hand and sat on the arm of the chair. The fire crackled, making popping noises as it dimmed. Together they watched it slowly die.

CHAPTER 13

Andy lifted the ringing phone and was surprised and glad to hear his father's voice.

"Andy," Max Taylor sounded jubilant. "It's Max. How are you?"

"I'm fine Max. How are you?"

"Okay. I'm okay. Can I see you? I want to talk to you."

"Sure, Max. Any time you say."

"Right now. Can you see me today?" Max sounded anxious, hurried.

"Well, yes. I guess. Where are you? I'll meet you."

"No. I'll come to you. You're sure you're free? This won't take long."

"Yes, I'm sure. I'd love to see you."

"I'll be there in a half hour or so."

Andy laid the phone in its cradle and turned to face Josie Monroe, the part-owner of The Exemplar Gallery. Not only did she handle Andy's work, she also was his love interest. Josie was at least ten years Andy's senior but she ignored his comments that he was far too young for her. She proved her commitment to him both in bed and in her gallery. Andy considered himself lucky that he had met her. She was not only the first gallery owner to accept his paintings, she was the only one.

"Who was that?" she asked.

"My father, Max Taylor. He's coming here."

So, Josie thought, she finally gets to meet the famous Maxwell Taylor.

"I'd better leave," she said. "You'll want to be alone with him. I'll be in the way."

"No. Not at all," Andy replied, saying exactly what she hoped he would say. "Don't worry about Max. He'll love you. It'll be good for you to meet him."

*   *   *

Andy opened the front door and Max entered the loft for the first time since Andy had moved in. Max looked paler. He seemed older than when Andy had seen him last. His hair was now completely white and his eyes seemed gray and drawn. When Max spoke, though, the fleeting impression of aging was gone and he once again became the person who lived in Andy's memory.

"How the hell are you?" Max said.

"Come in, Max," Andy said, ushering his father in.

Max saw Josie standing in the center of the room, surrounded by Andy's colorful paintings. She was holding a cup of coffee in one hand, standing in a slightly relaxed pose, her weight shifted onto one leg. The symmetrical, flowing lines of her disciplined body against the dramatic blaze of color momentarily startled Max.

"Well, well," he said smiling. "Just who is this delightful creature?"

"This is Josie Monroe, Max," Andy said. "Josie, this is my father, Max Taylor. Josie owns the Exemplar Gallery, uptown. She handles my work."

"Isn't that nice," Max offered, "to be represented by such a charming person?"

"Why thank you, Mr. Taylor. I've heard quite a bit about you," Josie replied, trying to sound gracious.

"All good, I hope," Max said.

"What's going on, Max? You sounded anxious." Andy asked after Max had seated himself and lit the inevitable cigarette. He did not deceive himself. It had to be about Alaska.

"It's about the hunt. Giff spoke to you about it?"

"Yes, he did."

"This is a bad time, I suppose," Max said glancing at Josie. "Perhaps I should come back another time."

"No," Andy said. "Feel free. Josie is like family."

"Really," Max said, glancing at her, momentarily embarrassing her with what she read in his eyes. She decided instantly to stay.

"Look," Max continued. "I've been waiting for word from Giff if you are going with us. He hasn't heard from you. And I've got to know, son. Time is running out."

"I don't know, Max," Andy retorted. "Josie is having a showing of my paintings in a few weeks. Time is running out for me too."

"Time," Max muttered, a cloud passing over his eyes. "Damned elusive thing."

Andy wasn't sure what Max meant by the remark. He assumed Max implied he was reaching the end of his days while Andy had years left in which to work. Andy was torn with the sudden desire to please Max and fulfill his wish to be with him. After all, there would be plenty of tomorrows for him to paint.

"Don't let the show stand in the way," Josie said. "We can postpone it."

"You've sent out the invitations," Andy said. "And what about the publicity? The brochures you've printed?"

"We can print new ones," Josie said.

"There, you see," Max interjected. "Josie won't stop you from joining us."

"It's not my decision," Josie said. "I'm just saying that the show date is not cut in concrete."

"It may be the last hunt we'll have together," Max said solemnly. "But I don't want to stand in your way. And I don't want to beg you."

But he was begging him, Andy thought. He'd never seen Max like this. He almost sounded desperate.

"You see these paintings, Max?" Andy said. "I've got a little over two weeks to get them to the gallery. I've got to finish the one there on the easel there and I must complete at least one more. If I work day and night, I might just make the deadline for the opening."

"We won't be leaving for at least three weeks," Max said.

"I won't be in any condition to go on a hunt then? How do you think I'll feel if the paintings don't sell? Do you want a depressed hunter with you? I might cause an accident."

"I have faith in you, Andy. I always had. You'll finish the work and it will sell. Anyone would want to buy these paintings."

Andy knew that Max, like Giff, did not appreciate nor understand art and neither man was sympathetic to Andy's obsession with painting. He knew he was being patronized right now.

"I hope so," Andy said. "I would hate to think that all this effort was in vain."

"Work," Max said somewhat profoundly, "is never in vain."

*　*　*

Later, when Max left and Andy picked up his palette, dabbing routinely at the canvas in front of him, Josie stood beside him.

"I want you to go with them," she said quietly.

"Really," Andy said.

"Yes. Really. I think you should go with your brother and father."

"Are you serious? I can't leave now. A trip like that could easily take a week or two. I've got to get this work done for you."

"You'll finish on time," Josie insisted. "Work day and night. You don't have to do another large canvas. Just finish this one. We can fill in with some of your smaller canvases and some watercolors."

"Damn, Josie. I don't know. We were never planning on variety. The theme was to be labor toiling . . . large canvases."

"We've got plenty of your paintings to mount a good show. Can't you see how important the hunt means to your father? He was pleading with you. I could see tears in his eyes."

Tears, Andy thought, were never a word in Max's lexicon.

"It must mean an awful lot to him, this trip. He said it might be his last. I don't think it would be wise to disappoint him. Why hurt him? He is your father."

"I'll tell you what," Andy responded. "If the show sells well, I'll go. The hunt is a couple of weeks after the show opening. I'll leave it up to your planning and I'll finish just this one painting."

"Good," Josie said. "I'll arrange everything. I'm positive the show will be a success."

"I'm afraid I don't quite have your faith," Andy said. "It's too difficult to guess what people want."

"Even your father knows what will sell," Josie said.

"You and he make a good team," Andy said. "A pair of optimists."

Yes, Josie thought, we would make a good team.

*   *   *

Max Taylor was surprised when he got the phone call from Josie Monroe. He grasped the phone and pressed it eagerly to his ear.

"What can I do for you?" he asked pleasantly.

"Mr. Taylor," Josie said. "Is it possible for me to speak to you privately?" Max thought he hadn't heard a voice so soft and refined since his wife, Ellen, had been his young bride.

"Call me Max," he said. "Only my enemies call me Mr. Taylor. Of course we can have a private conversation. Talk away."

"Not on the phone. Can I meet you somewhere privately? And I would like this to be strictly between you and me."

"Certainly, my dear. Sounds sinister. But I know just the place."

Max met her in a small out-of-the-way restaurant on Second Avenue where he stopped once in a while with a female companion.

"What's so important and secretive?" Max asked her once they had settled down at a booth. He was completely fascinated by this interesting woman. If Andy wasn't in her life, he thought, he might make a move on her.

"I'm pretty sure I can get Andy to go with you on your trip to Alaska," Josie said.

Max's face broke into a broad smile. "Bless you," he exclaimed. "How?"

"I know how much it means to you for him to go. I can see how much you care about him. And I want you to be happy."

"Yes?"

"Andy said he will go if he has a good sale at the show. He hasn't sold much so far and he has been dependent on you to a great degree."

"Andy doesn't have to worry about earning a living," Max told her. "He knows that. There's no need for him to struggle."

"But he wants to succeed as a painter. He wants his efforts to count."

"I've gathered that," Max said. "What is the point here?"

"If Andy's show is successful, if he sells well, he will feel that he has accomplished what he set out to do. I know he will go with you then."

A sly smile cracked the corners of Max Taylor's mouth. She is a fox, he thought. Why hadn't he thought of such a simple solution?

"Did he tell you that for sure?" Max asked.

"Yes. He'll go after the show. He told me that. But only if it is successful. If it should fail he'll probably withdraw and dig into his painting again. Start over."

"Does he know you came to see me?" Max asked, knowing that he didn't.

"No," Josie answered. "He would never allow me to see you."

"All right then," Max said boldly. "Let me take a wild guess. You want me to buy all of his paintings. Is that right?"

"Yes. But Andy would get suspicious if one person bought all his work. Or if your company bought them. That wouldn't look right. Could you arrange for their purchases to be spread out?"

"No problem. But aren't you afraid he may find out you're doing this?" Max asked.

"Yes. I've considered it. But we'll make sure he will never find out. Won't we, Max?" she said slyly.

"You're damned right," Max replied.

*   *   *

Andy was astounded that his paintings sold so well and brought in over sixty-two thousand dollars. After the gallery's share and expenses Andy would net half. He shared the space with two other artists and he believed it was just as well since he did not have enough work available to pull off a one-man show. Maybe in a couple of years, he mused. Every painting went to a number of unrelated buyers, from individuals to private collectors to corporate collections. He was overwhelmed by his instant success. He had gone into the show with a head full of doubts about his subject matter and even his ability to paint. Now, after such startling results, his doubts were allayed.

The reality of this newfound fortune was that he had labored for well over a year on the paintings that had sold. He had poured countless hours of energy and creative effort into them. He had paid for canvases, paints, stretchers, brushes, thinners, varnishes; all the paraphernalia that goes with the work. For all this effort he had earned about what he made waiting tables. But he didn't accept earnings as a factor. It was the future that mattered. The price per painting would increase along with his reputation and the money would come.

Now he was ready to accept Max's invitation to join the hunt.

* * *

The pickets were still in front of the building. They had not given up. Max wondered what their ultimate intentions were. Did they intend to wreck Taylor Cosmetics? Did they want to close the company down? Bankruptcy? Were these people anti-capitalist, a new bastion of communism? What was it they sought?

Maybe Giff was right. Maybe going public was the answer. Having thousands of shareholders with the interests of the company at heart might be the way to combat the onslaught of radicals who did not. His thoughts were interrupted by his secretary's buzz. Andy was calling. Max eagerly put the phone to his ear.

"Yes, Andy," he said.

"Max," Andy said softly, "I hope you'll forgive me for the way I've been lately." There was a trace of emotion in his voice. Max braced himself for bad news.

"Forgive you?" Max said. "For what?"

"I haven't been pleasant to talk to. I didn't mean to put you off. I want you to know I am going with you and Giff to Alaska."

Max smiled. His voice sounded his joy. "I'm so glad, Andy. This is wonderful news."

"I must be crazy," Andy said. "Hunting wolves in Alaska. I'm not a hunter."

"It'll be great," Max assured him. "Just like the old days. You'll have a great time with us."

"Sure, Max," Andy said. "I'm already glad."

"I'll have the law department take care of the permits. I'll get in touch with you as soon as everything is worked out and arrangements are made. I want you to call Giff and work out details for gear and equipment you will need."

"Okay, Max."

"How did the exhibit go?" Max asked, keeping his voice level, not to reveal the fact that he knew the results.

"Very well," Andy responded. "As a matter of fact, it practically sold out."

"That's great, son. You're on the way to becoming a big name as an artist. People will call me Andy Foster's father."

"We'll see."

"How's Josie?"

"Fine. She's quite a woman."

"Yes," Max said. "That she is. Quite a woman."

PART THREE

CHAPTER 14

Charles W. Fairbanks, Vice-President of the United States under Theodore Roosevelt, bore the distinction of having his name preserved for posterity. The city of Fairbanks was named after Mr. Fairbanks, an honor diminished only by the fact that, in contrast, the capital city of the state of Alaska, Juneau, derived its name from a personage of no such high office. Joseph Juneau was merely a prospector who found gold near the site of the now capital city.

The second-largest city in Alaska, Fairbanks is situated well into the interior. The Arctic Circle is no more than one hundred and fifty miles north.

Coffin took a cab from the airport and walked along Cushman Street in downtown Fairbanks. It was the end of the Winter Carnival and there was activity all through the city. The Championship Sled Dog Races would soon be started and there was excitement everywhere. He thought of this time two years ago, when he and Lucy had come to town to enjoy the festivities. He had mentioned to her at the time, that it was too bad they didn't have wolf sled racing. How strange that idea seemed now.

The wolf pack he believed he controlled had betrayed him in

an instant. How much did he really know about these animals, he wondered. Everything he had learned about them now served only one purpose: to track them.

He was here to learn something of the men he was to accompany on their hunt. As convinced as he was that he would eventually find and kill Midnight, he was likewise unconvinced that he should become a guide to men who were here for the same ultimate purpose as his. He was sorry now that he had committed to the hunt. But he would honor that commitment. He obtained from Jim Fuller the names of the hunters and where they would be staying.

He sat at the bar in the North Star Hotel, labeled by its owner as "the best in the north." He easily picked out his group as three men who were sitting at a table having dinner. The room was large, with low ceilings, a combination bar and restaurant. Completely finished in heavy, dark wood, it created a rustic mood one might expect in the region. There was nothing slick or modern about the style; all detail was muted and understated. The lighting was soft, the accents enhancing the rough textures of the wood. On the walls, placed at various focal points, were mounted heads of caribou, elk and moose. On the wall near the end of the bar hung one of the most outstanding trophies. It was the complete pelt of a very large wolf, cut open and laid out flat, the legs spread like the points of a star. The huge head was intact and the jaws were propped open, the jagged teeth bared in a permanent snarl. The glass eyes gleamed red.

The men were involved in heavy conversation, some of which reached Coffin's ears.

"Goddamn!" Giff said to the men at the table. "Will you look at that prize!" He pointed to the wolf on the wall. All heads turned in the direction he had indicated.

"Magnificent beast, isn't it?" Max Taylor said.

"That's what I'm after," Giff said. "One trophy like that and this trip will be worth it."

"Think we'll get one that big?" Max asked.

"Why not?" Giff responded. "We'll just keep hunting until we do."

"Might take longer than we have time," Max said. "I don't think they normally come that big."

"Probably not," Giff said. "But the range we'll be hunting on has an unlimited quota on wolves. You can shoot as many as you want. We'll hunt until we get what we want. One as big as that." He pointed to the hanging pelt.

"Is that legal?" Andy questioned. "No limit."

"Sure it's legal," Giff said. "I checked. There are some areas where the limit is two to four wolves. And there are others where there is no limit. We're going to one of those."

"Isn't one wolf enough for a trophy?" Andy asked.

"Sure," Giff replied. "One is enough. If it's like that one on the wall. He must have weighed almost a couple of hundred pounds."

The men stared at the wolf, contemplating Giff's remark.

"How far do we travel from here, Giff?" Andy asked.

"We get a chartered plane in the morning. All the gear will be loaded on for us. We go inland for a few hundred miles to a town called Fort Yukon. And here is where it gets tricky. We meet a guy there who will take us farther inland. We stay at a lodge he owns. That is where our main camp will be. We hunt wolves from there with snowmobiles and shotguns."

"Snowmobiles," Andy said. "What do we know about handling snowmobiles?"

"What's to know?" Giff said. "We'll spend a few hours practicing before we actually hunt from them."

"We're not exactly going to be joyriding," Andy said. "We're going into the wolf's environment. To kill him. Don't you think he's going to fight back?"

"What the hell can wolves do against us?" Giff said. "They don't stand a chance. I did some research. I talked to the guides up there. The snowmobiles can easily run a wolf down in deep snow. The guides will go with us. One guy rides behind the driver with a shotgun. We can't miss."

"As simple as that?" Andy said.

"Hell, it's easy," Giff said. "We've been in much tougher situations in the past. Remember that black bear in Canada, Max? Just you and me alone when that son-of-a-bitch comes charging out of the woods from nowhere. We got him."

"You got him, you mean," Max said. "If you hadn't whipped off three fast shots he would have batted my head into the next state without the rest of me."

"But, listen," Giff said. "Wolves aren't like that. I mean, they won't attack us. They'll run from us. Basically, they are cowards. They're afraid of man."

"I hope the wolves know they're supposed to be afraid of us," Andy said, a ring of sarcasm in his voice.

Giff ignored his comment. "I have no doubts," Giff said. "We'll have a good hunt. I'd rather shoot them from a moving plane, but that's outlawed."

"I'm still wondering why we have to kill wolves to begin with," Andy said.

"Damn it, Andy!" Giff cried. "Just look at that creature on the wall. How can you ask a question like that? Just the fact that it can be done. To know that a man can take out a beast like that. That's reason enough."

Andy didn't push Giff. He didn't want to argue with him. There was no point causing a disagreement so early on the trip. He knew he shouldn't have come. He didn't belong here. He was always the outsider. He was here only to placate Max.

"Well," Max said. "I, for one, would love to bag a wolf like that one on the wall. But any wolf would suit me fine."

By eleven that night Giff and Andy were alone at the bar. Max had left his sons and had gone to bed. It was an opportunity Andy waited for all day, to privately ask Giff about something that had been bothering him since the trip began.

"Giff," he said, "is there anything wrong with Max?"

"Like what, kid?"

"I'm not sure. It's nothing I can pin down. I haven't seen him

in a while. I feel . . . I don't know. He's just not the same Max. I
see something in his eyes. A weariness. He seems preoccupied at
times. Far away. He isn't sick, is he?"

"Not that I know of," Giff lied. Why should Andy know?

"He doesn't seem slower than normal to you?"

"I hadn't noticed. But I see him all the time. What the
hell, Max is over seventy. You don't expect him to look the
same all the time, do you? He's probably just showing his age
a little, is all."

"I hope you're right," Andy said. "I'm not sure he's up to this
hunt business."

"Believe me, kid, Max is as healthy as a horse. Don't worry
about him," Giff said. "Max will be leading us all. He'll probably
get the first kill."

Andy smiled and sipped what remained of his drink. He wasn't
convinced by Giff's casualness. Giff turned his attention away from
Andy and his eyes rested again on the magnificent wolf pelt. Giff
motioned to the bartender for another round of drinks. The man
behind the counter brought them and spoke to Giff. "I understand you guys are going on a wolf hunt."

"That's right," Giff said. "Who told you?"

"Word gets around," the man said. He was middle-aged, concrete gray hair, slightly built. A handlebar mustache completely
covered his upper lip and when he talked it looked like he didn't
move his lips.

"You know much about wolves?" Giff asked. "Maybe you could
give us a few pointers."

"Not me," the bartender said. He turned and pointed to a
man standing at the other end of the bar. "There's the man you
want to talk to. He's a wolf hunter."

Giff and Andy looked to where the bartender had indicated.
Standing alone at the end of the bar was Miles Coffin.

"Name's Miles Coffin," the bartender said.

"Think he might have a drink with us?" Giff asked.

"Why don't you ask him?"

"Send him down one," Giff said. "And let him know we'd like him to join us."

The bartender nodded, poured a scotch and took it to the other end of the bar. He deposited it in front of Coffin and he briefly spoke to him. Within a minute the hunter left his spot and walked over to Giff and Andy.

"Thanks for the drink," the wolf hunter said.

"Join us, please," Giff said.

Miles Coffin slipped into a seat beside the two men.

"What can I do for you gents?" Coffin asked. "Bartender said you wanted to chat."

"My name is Giff Taylor," Giff said, extending his hand to Coffin. "This is Andy Foster."

"I'm Miles Coffin," the lean, bearded hunter said.

"Wolves," Giff said. "We're here to hunt wolves."

"I heard," Coffin said.

"We'd like to talk to you about wolves," Giff said. "I understand you've hunted them."

"Some," Coffin replied. "What would you like to know?"

"Anything we could use," Giff said. "How big are they generally?"

"Anywhere from about sixty pounds to one hundred forty or so, some larger."

"How large?" Andy said.

"The largest might be around one seventy five, but that weight is rare," Coffin said. "They don't usually come that big. But there have been some."

"How about the one on the wall there," Giff said, pointing to the mounted skin. "How much would you think he weighed?"

"He was around one fifty, I'd say."

"How can you be sure?" Giff said.

"I shot him," Coffin answered.

"I'll be damned," Giff exclaimed. "How'd you get him?"

"Shotgun. From a plane. That was over ten years ago. They don't allow hunting from planes anymore."

"Why the hell not?" Giff asked, already aware of the reasons. "That would be the best way to hunt wolves."

"It was too easy," Coffin answered. "Hunters killed too many."

Giff realized that the hunter was only responding to questions asked him specifically. He was not yet contributing any information Giff did not already know. In order to pick this man's brain he felt he would have to keep firing questions.

"We're hunting by snowmobile," Andy interjected. "Sounds kind of dangerous."

"It's done quite often," Coffin said. He drained the rest of his scotch and placed the empty glass on the bar, covering exactly the wet ring left by the glass he had been drinking. Giff signaled the bartender to refill the glass.

"Thanks," Coffin said, accepting the fresh drink.

"We won't have any trouble hunting from snowmobiles, will we?" Andy asked.

"Not generally," the wolfer replied. "But with wolves you never know."

"What do you mean by that?" Giff asked.

"They are extremely smart hunters. They won't let you kill them if they can avoid you. You've got to get lucky. Get them in the open. In the deep snow is best. If you can trap a pack in the open you'd have a good chance of running them down. They'll tire out and your machines won't. It's that simple."

This was more like it, Giff thought. He wanted this man's knowledge to pour out.

"Why do you hunt wolves?" Andy asked, his indirect question coming just when Coffin was opening up to his probing. Giff was annoyed. He didn't need Andy moralizing now.

"Predator control mostly," Coffin said. "The government paid me to trim the packs."

"How dangerous is it?" Giff interrupted. He wanted to get Coffin back on the details of hunting the wolves. "Hunting from snowmobiles. Have you ever done it?"

"I've killed some that way," Coffin confessed. "It's not very dangerous as long as you're armed and careful."

Coffin lifted the fresh glass of scotch to his lips and drained half in one gulp.

"It's our first wolf hunt," Andy said. "Will we have trouble? Being beginners, I mean."

"You shouldn't if you have good guides. They should compensate for your inexperience."

Giff felt slighted. He was suddenly considered a novice hunter because of Andy's statements. "We may not have hunted wolves," he said. "But I've hunted everything you can name. And I can tell you this, wolves die, just like any other animal. They can be blown away by a gun blast. I've brought down bigger and more dangerous game than wolves."

Coffin looked directly into Giff's eyes.

"First thing you do," he said icily, "is never underestimate your prey."

"From what I've heard," Giff said, "the wolf is a coward. He kills only when it's to his advantage and his prey is always the weaker one. He attacks in a pack to back him up. And, at the first sign of danger, he'll run."

"You happen to be also describing man," Coffin said. "What you say is true to a degree. You do have a few surprises coming. The wolf is not a coward. And he will attack and fight alone if he's forced to. A lone wolf can take down a full-grown moose."

"Crap," Giff said. "I don't buy that."

"A wolf can sleep through a blizzard," Coffin continued, undaunted. "He can run over a hundred miles without a rest. He can go days without water. He eats a third of his weight in one meal. He can pick up the scent of a prey for over a mile away. He is a relentless hunter who will wear his prey down until it drops from exhaustion no matter how big it is. He never gives up once he has made up his mind."

This was better, Giff thought. This guy was spilling it out now.

"You are partially right, though," Coffin continued. "The wolf does generally attack in a pack and he does make sure he has the advantage in a battle."

"And he's afraid of man," Giff said.

"Yes, he is," Coffin said. "Since the white man came to America he has killed the wolf with a passion. He brought the old-world hatred of the wolf with him and he never learned how to live with the animal and share nature like the Indian did. The white man has almost completely wiped them out in the mainland of the United States. Only Alaska and Canada are the last refuges for the wolf. He has run away from man."

"You see," Giff said. "Even you admit it. The wolf ran away from man."

"Wouldn't you run from someone who was determined to destroy you if you had no way to fight back?" Coffin asked.

Giff didn't answer.

"The wolf is the true hunter," Coffin continued speaking. "He hunts to live, to survive. He rarely kills without a reason."

"You sound like you have a fondness for wolves," Andy said to Coffin. "It's kind of difficult for me to picture you killing these animals, considering the way you've been praising them."

Coffin smiled. "A fondness? Perhaps."

"If the wolf is all you say he is, necessary in the balance of nature, then why is he still hunted and destroyed? He doesn't interfere with human civilization anymore," Andy said.

"He is game, like any other animal," Coffin said. "When the wolf overpopulates he will kill off too many deer, moose and caribou. He, in turn, is killed off so that the deer population is not depleted too quickly. It's a man-made balance of nature made to suit mankind."

"What exactly do you mean?" Andy asked, obviously fascinated.

"The hunter must have enough game to hunt," Coffin said, his voice steady, not caring if he was about to antagonize these hunters. "If the wolf is allowed to multiply and hunt indiscriminately, unchecked, he will reduce the game supply to the point that man will not have a sufficient supply to hunt. The wolf must be kept to a level of growth that will not interfere with man's need to hunt."

Giff was exasperated by now. "Are you saying that the wolf was slaughtered so that man would have enough game to hunt?" he said.

"That was not why he was initially slaughtered," Coffin answered. "At first he was destroyed because he interfered with the growth of civilization. As man moved across North America the wolf became his enemy. The wolf killed off the game and animals man needed to live; cattle, sheep. Man struck back at the wolf out of a fear that came from generations of superstitions and hatred of the wolf. He used traps, guns, poisons, anything he could think of to kill the wolf who dared interfere with his progress. But as he destroyed the wolf he also killed millions of wildlife."

"When was all this supposed to have happened?" Giff said sarcastically.

"Over the last few hundred years," Coffin replied. "But it really accelerated when the west was opened after the Civil War."

"It had to happen," Andy said. "How could a predator like the wolf exist alongside man as the human population grew?"

"Right," Coffin said. "Man is just as much a predator as the wolf. They became enemies competing for the same game. But the white man never tried to coexist with the wolf. He wanted to eliminate the wolf."

"Competition," Giff said. "Man eliminated his competition. No different than business. Survival of the fittest."

"Tell me," Coffin said, speaking directly to Giff, "why are you determined to hunt wolves? It's not like deer. You certainly can't eat the meat of a wolf."

Giff deliberated his answer for a moment. "For the sport," he said. "The hunt is a great sport."

"Is it really?" the wolf hunter asked. He finished his scotch and set the empty glass on the bar. The bartender was quick to refill it this time without Giff beckoning him.

"You're fucking right it is," Giff said. "The best sport because the wolf is a hunter being hunted. By man, the best hunter."

"Man began hunting to feed his belly," Coffin said. "Why does he hunt today? You say it's for sport. To collect trophies? Testimony of his prowess? To prove that he can kill animals? Here's the true sport in hunting; don't bring your guns or bows and arrows. No planes. No snowmobiles, jeeps. Just bring a knife. Go into the interior and hunt the wolf and try and take him on those terms, where the odds have been reduced and not in your favor."

"You know something," Giff challenged Coffin belligerently. "I'm beginning to doubt that you killed that wolf hanging on the wall. I'm thinking that you're actually one of those anti-hunting nuts who thinks of the animal world as a fairy-tale cartoon."

"Think what you like," Coffin said.

"For Christ sakes, Giff," Andy said. "Take it easy. This man is right."

"I'd expect you to sympathize with him," Giff scoffed. "Hunting was never your bag. But there are millions of hunters who feel the same way I do. Man is the best hunter because he has the brains to create weapons that prove he is better than the biggest animal alive. How could he fight a bear, or a moose, an elephant without his brain and weapons?"

"You got me wrong," Coffin said. "I'm certainly not anti-hunting."

"Then what the hell are you trying to say?" Giff swore.

"Only this. Hunting today has changed. It's not the same as it once was. The modern hunter is not motivated as his ancestors were. He has made hunting into a game between him and the animal. And the ultimate end of that game is that the animal must die for whatever the reason. Otherwise the game would not be complete."

"So hunting is a game," Giff said.

"That's what it has become," Coffin said. "There are few true hunters left today. The man who hunts solely for food and not for trophies is a true hunter. The wolf is the true hunter."

"He's a fucking scavenger," Giff cursed. "He deserves to be annihilated."

"What gives man the right to kill for no other reason than to satisfy his desire to kill?" Coffin said.

"What gives the wolf the right to kill?" Giff countered.

"Natural order. The wolf was given the tools to hunt for his food by nature. He fits into the order of things. He has stamina, daring, strength. And the teeth and jaws needed to kill his prey."

"And man has a brain," Giff whipped back. "And a gun . . ."

"Let me ask you something," Andy interrupted the banter between the two men. "If it isn't too personal. Just how many wolves did you kill?"

"I'm not sure. I never counted," Coffin said quickly and flatly. "An awful waste," he added.

Andy believed he saw a flash of pain in Coffin's expression. There was obviously something more to this man then he was witnessing tonight, he thought. And he would never know the complete man who had piqued his interest.

"So what?" Giff said. "So what if all those wolves died? What difference did it really make?"

"None, I suppose, that you'd notice," Coffin said. He drained the remainder of his drink and once again placed the glass over the ring on the bar. "Thank you gents for the drinks," he said. "I wish you luck on your hunt." He turned instantly and walked out of the bar without another word.

The two men watched him leave.

"That is a strange man," Andy said.

"He's a goddamn phony," Giff stated. "Did he expect us to buy that crap about killing so many wolves that he lost count? Who'd he think he was talking to? That was bullcrap for the naive mainland city folk. He got what he was after, some free drinks."

"I suppose," Andy muttered.

When the bartender came by again Andy spoke to him. "Tell me," he said, "that man Coffin—do you know him well?"

"Only slightly."

"Is it true that he killed a lot of wolves?"

"It sure is," the man answered.

"You wouldn't happen to know how many?" Giff asked.

"I couldn't say for sure. But from what I hear it's got to be about a thousand, more or less."

CHAPTER 15

In the battle with the great bull moose, one of the attacking wolves who died was Moon's second surviving male offspring. Of her first litter there remained now only one male and the female. The male, like his father, was a ferocious hunter, quickly learning the ways of survival. He had not grown nearly as large as his sire, yet he was unafraid to attack large game. The female followed her mother's lead and stayed out of the thick of attack. She tended to be cautious. She too had learned well, and, like her mother, was a good hunter when required. She would join in the attack when called upon to assist.

The pack returned to their lairs and slept and played for days until the pangs of hunger returned and the cycle continued. The pack reassembled and set out once again upon the unending trek through their territory. When they crossed the scene of the encounter with the great moose they found the carcasses of the fallen pack members had been partially eaten by predators. The pack quickly devoured the remains of the dead wolves, leaving behind only pelts and skeletons.

This winter had not been overly severe. The wolves were not starving. The storehouses still contained food. Game was available, although not plentiful, in this milder than normal winter. Many caribou were spotted wandering through the territory feeding on lichens and saplings.

But it was early March and the winter was not over. Although there were fewer major storms than normal there were still more than two months of cold weather to go before the first traces of milder temperatures would come. The pack could never delay in their quest for nourishment. They must be relentless hunters, never ceasing their unending search for food.

A serious storm struck while the pack was on the trail of a herd of caribou. It came suddenly and without warning. It was a furious storm, driven by gale-force winds. The snow quickly piled up in large drifts and it became extremely difficult for the animals to navigate in the blinding downfall. They were in the open without protection when it hit in its fury. They had to regroup and thrust their way through the blizzard to the safety of surrounding woodlands. The blinding force confused them and some members of the pack strayed. Visibility was cut and the fierce wind made it impossible to retain the scent of the pack. Midnight led most of the wolves into a cluster of low-hanging spruce and there they spent the night. Under the shelter of the thick trees, the wolves curled up into individual balls, tucking their muzzles under their hind legs. Their thick fur would protect them from the blizzard and keep them warm.

Midnight's remaining male offspring was one of the wolves who had become separated from the pack. He might have found shelter but Midnight could not risk finding him and guiding him back to the pack. The younger wolf would have to take care of himself. If he survived the night, he would catch up to the other wolves when the storm subsided.

Midnight had no way of knowing the yearling's plight at the moment. The younger, less experienced wolf had been cut off and was completely disoriented. He had lost the scent of the pack and could not regain his sense of direction. In the raging storm, he had wandered onto the edge of a small lake which had only recently frozen over. Stepping on a thin spot in the snow-covered ice, his weight broke through and he fell into water over his head. He struggled desperately to find purchase on the slippery surface. The weight of the water in his fur was dragging him under. After a desperate struggle to stay afloat, he finally managed to get a hind paw onto the ice. He painfully pulled himself to the surface, quickly shaking off most of the water, which was already freezing in his fur. His coat was a mass of small icicles as he crawled away from the hole, back in the direction he had come. They hung from his ears, tail and even his eyelids.

He followed his own rapidly disappearing paw prints in the surface of the snow to where he felt the ground was firm. He found the shelter of a group of rocks and curled up against them. He tucked his muzzle under his hind quarters and closed his eyes. Soon he fell asleep while the storm raged around him. He would be completely protected from the blizzard by the thick fur on his body. His only vulnerable spot was his nose, but, instinctively his legs and tail curled over it, keeping it warm. When the storm dissipated, he would break the snow from his body and seek out the pack.

*   *   *

The blizzard broke during the night, leaving behind a foot of soft snow that would make hunting difficult for the pack in the coming weeks. Even their storehouses would not be easy to locate, their scent markings buried under the drifts.

The young wolf awoke and pulled his head out from between his legs. He was covered by a drift of snow and his coat had frozen over with a thin layer of ice. He stood up and pulled himself out of the snow bank, cracking the ice covering on his fur. He shook the white powder from his body and moved out into the virgin snow. His tracks from the night before had completely disappeared.

There was no sign of the pack, but the air was still and he would be able to pick up their scent if they were not too far away.

He was within the confines of the pack's territory and eventually he would join up with them.

It was the first time he had been separated from the pack since he was born. There had always been one of the adults nearby to watch and protect him. This was his first chance to prove he had matured and that he could find his way back to the pack on his own.

He was not hungry, having eaten with the pack recently, but he would be within a few days. He broke through the freshly fallen snow, heading away from the lake, staying along the edge of the forest. His course was difficult and slow. He was not making good time and by mid-morning he had detected no sign of the pack.

He finally caught their scent after he had traveled two miles along the rim of the forest. The wolves were at least a mile ahead of him on the other side of a glade. He did not see them but he was downwind and their scent was unmistakable. He set out across the open expanse of the glade to join with them.

He saw two gray wolves, about a quarter of a mile away, heading in the same direction. He recognized them as subordinate wolves from the pack who, like himself, became separated during the storm. The wolves moved slowly through the deep snow, relentlessly pressing forward. On the other side of the clearing they finally saw the pack who had forsaken the sanctuary of the woods and had moved into the open to rejoin the strays. To the south another gray wolf appeared. All moved toward the center of the glade where they would converge and join up.

Midnight, followed by Moon, led the remaining members of the pack towards a rendezvous with the strays. The four separate parties aimed at a point in the white blanket where they would meet. The trail they left loosely resembled the spokes of a wheel that met at the hub. The ground they covered was deep with the new snow and it took the wolves a long time before they were finally together.

With Moon setting the mood, the pack nestled close to her male offspring and the other lost members. The wolves licked their faces in greeting and nestled close to each other. Then they began a series of howls that shattered the still, cold day. They brayed in harmony, each sending out cries that hung in the air for long seconds, joining the other howls and creating a weird cacophony of eerie sounds.

They followed Midnight in a long single file. He led the way, breaking the ground for the pack, who trailed in his paw prints.

Suddenly, the wolves froze in their tracks. A loud, rumbling noise split the air, like the roar of a strange giant beast. It was a continuous noise that did not cease. There was no pause. It was a constant sound that ripped at their hearts. The noise came closer, ever closer. The wolves all looked upward as the sound grew louder and came from just above them in the air. In utter terror, they saw a giant bird swoop down out of the sky, its wings stretched out straight from both sides. There were strange markings on its body and wings. Its eyes were hollow, large and transparent. None of the wolves had ever been so close to this large birdlike creature that roared above them.

Only Midnight, who had lived in the world of men, sensed that man had entered the pack's territory and would soon make an impact on the lives of all the wolves.

CHAPTER 16

The lodge was located eighty miles northeast of Fort Yukon, deep into the interior of the Alaska back country. The plane Giff had scheduled at a Fairbanks flying service flew them the rest of the way to the lodge. It was a twin-engine Cessna. Max and Andy sat side by side in the back while Giff dozed in front next to the pilot.

"Did you ever see such magnificent country?" Max said to Andy, his head turned away towards the window.

"It is spectacular," Andy admitted. "I just hope we can handle it."

"Are you worried?" Max asked, his attention directed back to his son.

"No. At least not yet," Andy said softly. He did not want Giff to hear him. He had enough of Giff's cynicism in Fairbanks. There was a point reached back there when Andy feared a fight might have broken out between Giff and the strange hunter, Coffin.

"Are you sorry you came?" Max asked.

"No," Andy replied. "I'm happy to be with you, Max. I think this trip might be good for us."

Max rested his hand on Andy's. "There's so much I've wanted to say to you. We never seem to have the time. Perhaps now . . ."

But suddenly there was that same distant, foreign expression on Max's face again. It came quickly, as if prompted by a thought that lay back in his mind and emerged like a phantom.

"Is everything all right, Max?" Andy said, obvious concern in his voice.

"Yes," Max was quick to reply. "Of course. What makes you think there's something wrong?"

"I'm sorry," Andy said. "It's just that you seemed suddenly preoccupied. I thought something might be . . . worrying you."

"No. Just a lot on my mind, is all. I'm not getting any younger. No man likes to think of his life as winding down. It's not like it used to be. This may be our last hunt together . . . you, me and Giff. I don't know if I'll be up to it in a few years. Maybe I'm just getting more sentimental than I ever admitted to myself."

Andy had never heard Max speak of his age before, or recognition of his own mortality. It was out of character for him. He had always behaved as if he would live forever. Now this.

"I'm glad you wanted me to come," Andy said.

*   *   *

The Cessna landed on a snow-covered clearing that served as an airstrip, its skis touching down perfectly on the uncertain runway. The temperature was fourteen degrees and the sun was shining brightly when the hunting party emerged from the plane. They were met by two men who had parked two four-by-fours on a narrow road that ran parallel to the airfield. The men were from the lodge.

"My name is Jim Fuller," one of the men said. "This is my partner, Willie Mason."

"I'm Max Taylor," Max said and introduced Giff and Andy.

They watched the small plane take off and disappear out of sight over the ridge of timber.

They loaded the gear into the vehicles and split into two groups. They were driven another thirty miles north to the lodge.

Giff was in the first vehicle while Andy and Max sat in the second. The road they traveled was, they soon discovered, not much of a road at all. It was more a trail that had been cleared. The going was rough as the four-by-four bounced along, jostling its passengers. Andy noticed Max was holding up well along the way so far. His father grimaced noticeably at times but remained silent, keeping his feelings to himself.

"How was the trip up from Fairbanks?" Fuller asked.

"All right," Andy replied. "Pretty smooth."

"Well, you're lucky," Fuller said. "The weather is on your side right now. We had a storm a few days ago. Left about a foot of new snow and a lot of ice."

"It's not that cold," Andy said. "I thought it would be a lot colder up here. But it actually feels like New York in January."

"It's the end of winter," Fuller said. "The best time to hunt wolves. You couldn't hunt in December and January. Gets down to forty below at times. Even the animals have it rough. No food. Everything frozen solid. We still get some pretty cold weather this time of year though."

"How will the hunting be?" Max asked. "Will we have any trouble with the new snow?"

"Not at all," Fuller said. "In fact, the snow will work in your favor. The wolves have difficulty moving in the deep snow. The snowmobiles we'll use can easily overrun them. If we can force a pack into the open we should have a good chance to get a few."

"How many snowmobiles do you have at the lodge?" Max asked.

"We've got more than enough. Six. But the way we'll work is this; there are five of us now. We have another guide coming in the morning. We'll take three machines. Two men on each. One man driving and one man riding shotgun. If Miles Coffin doesn't show up we'll have to rotate on the machines."

"What was that name you just said?" Andy asked, surprised, not sure that he had heard correctly.

"Coffin. Miles Coffin," Fuller said.

"Well I'll be damned," Andy said.

"Do you know Coffin?" Fuller asked.

"I met him for the first time the other night in Fairbanks," Andy said. "We talked about hunting wolves."

"That's just like Coffin," the driver said. "He was probably looking your group over before he came on out here."

"Didn't he tell you who he was?" Max asked, curious.

"No," Andy said. "He just talked about hunting and wolves."

"And he didn't tell you he was our guide?" Max grunted. "Why would he do something like that?"

"Well, knowing Coffin," Jim Fuller said, "I'd say he wanted to feel you out a little. He's very particular about who he's going out on a hunt with."

"So he was checking us out," Andy said.

"I guess so."

"He's got some damn nerve," Max said. "I don't care for that kind of crap. I'm paying for a guide, I expect a guide. Not some bastard scrutinizing me."

"Coffin is the best, Mr. Taylor," Fuller said. "He may seem a little peculiar but he makes it easier for us on a hunt. Knows exactly what wolves will do."

Andy saw the disgruntled expression on Max's face and knew he was not satisfied with the man's answer. But he didn't belabor the point. Max didn't like anyone questioning his motivation.

"I heard that Coffin personally killed hundreds of wolves," Andy said. "Can that be true?"

"Oh, it's true all right," the driver said. "Miles, he has a big reputation in these parts. Goes back twenty years or so. Best wolf hunter in the interior at one time. In those days Coffin and a lot of wolfers used to kill the wolves from planes. It wasn't too hard to kill off quite a few that way. But the wolf is protected from wholesale slaughter now."

"Aren't wolves an endangered species?" Andy asked.

"Not up here, they're not. In the rest of the States, yes. But not in Alaska and Canada. The wolf has moved north. Up here, especially in the interior, he is fair game. There are many hunters who just out-and-out hate wolves. They come here to destroy them. Not just to hunt them but to actually wipe them out."

"Did Coffin intend to stop us if he didn't approve of us?" Andy said.

"I don't know," Jim Fuller said. "I have no idea what Coffin might do."

*   *   *

The lodge was a two-storied cabin built of hand-hewn logs. It was set back off the bumpy road in a small clearing that had obviously been hacked out of the woods which surrounded it. The lodge was framed by huge snowcapped pines, which complemented the rustic atmosphere.

The two vehicles pulled up in front of the building and the men unloaded their gear. The luggage included guns, ammunition, cold-weather clothing, boots, gloves, snowshoes. The men carried the equipment into the cabin. Andy watched Max struggle with a pack and took it from him. Max would have normally fought him, but, curiously, his father didn't object.

Andy was pleasantly surprised that the interior of the building was so much larger than it appeared from the outside. The main room was dominated by a massive stone fireplace that occupied one entire wall and ran up to the roof joints. Large, open beams braced the ceilings and ran across the room, joining one wall and the balcony that led to the sleeping quarters.

Directly under the balcony was a long bar made from thick pine logs. Behind the bar two doors were cut into a wall that separated the kitchen and bathrooms from the main room. Shelves on the wall behind the bar testified to an ample supply of liquor. On the wall opposite the bar hung a gun rack with a dozen shotguns and at least as many combinations of rifles.

The bags were dropped in the middle of the room and the

men immediately assembled at the bar. The two drivers hung their jackets in a large closet near the entrance. Jim Fuller took a position behind the bar.

"You guys have the complete run of the place," Fuller said. "Sleeping quarters upstairs. Bathrooms and kitchen behind us. The bar is open all the time. We have no bartenders. You just help yourselves."

"Nice place. You've done some good work here," Giff said. "Did you build it?"

"No," Fuller answered. "We bought it from a hunter's family. He died and they had no use for it. We modernized it. Put in new bathrooms and expanded and updated the kitchen. The fireplace and sleeping rooms were part of the original structure."

"Good job," Giff said. "Get many customers?"

"We have clients here most of the year. We shut down only in the really severe winter months. Nobody hunts then."

"I'm hungry as hell," Giff changed the subject. "I guess everybody else is too."

"There's steaks and trimmings," Fuller said. "We'll rustle up a batch in a minute." His hand was on a bottle of Johnny Walker when he spoke. "What'll you gents have?"

"What you got there is fine for me," Giff said.

The men shed their coats, hats and gloves and joined the partners at the bar. As they were drinking Andy brought up the subject of Miles Coffin.

"Giff," he said to his half brother, "Remember the guy we met in the hotel bar in Fairbanks? Miles Coffin."

"Sure, why wouldn't I remember him?" Giff said. "The bullcrap hunter."

"I've never heard him called that before," Fuller said.

"You won't believe this but he is supposed to show up here as our guide," Andy said.

"What?" Giff was incredulous. "Is that right?" he said to Fuller. "You hired that anti-hunting nut as our guide."

"I've never known Coffin to be anti-hunting," Fuller said. "I don't know what he said that would give you that impression but he has always been an excellent guide for us. One of the best I know."

"Well, I hope he changes his attitude when he gets here," Giff said. "He sounded like he was carrying some kind of chip on his shoulder when we met him."

"He may not even show up," Andy said. "We're not sure he approved of us. Isn't that right?" he asked Fuller.

"It's possible," Fuller replied. "But not likely. But don't worry. We should have good luck even if he can't make it. There's a fresh snowfall and the weather's holding up."

"Then what the hell do we need Coffin for?" Giff said.

"He's the extra edge," Fuller replied. "He saves time out there."

"Time we have plenty of," Giff said.

"Do we get a chance to ride those snowmobiles before we go out after the wolves?" Max asked. "Might be a good idea. We need practice."

"Sure," Fuller said. "After we eat we'll spend a little time running you guys around so you get the feel of the machines."

"When do we actually start hunting?" Max Taylor said.

"At dawn," Fuller said. "We can't hunt today. The law states that any hunter arriving by plane cannot hunt until the day following his arrival."

"I'll be damned," Giff said. "Why?"

"It's to assure that he has not hunted by plane," Fuller said. "The Game and Fish Department is very strict about the use of planes to hunt game."

"What if you do and you get caught?" Giff asked.

"The fines are steep," Fuller said. "And they will confiscate the hunter's plane."

"Damn," Giff exclaimed. "That's pretty rough for just killing an animal."

"Yeh. It's a big price to pay. You won't find much hunting by plane anymore. It's just not worth it," Fuller told them.

"Too bad," Giff said.

* * *

Giff and Andy took turns alternating driving positions on the snowmobiles for the remainder of the afternoon. Max stayed behind, determined that he would not be put in the position of driver. Fuller asserted that all the men going on the hunt should learn to handle the machines, but Max was adamant. He knew he might not be dependable in a bad situation. Giff agreed with Fuller but, knowing Max's condition, would not push his father on the issue. Max's attitude was that of a troubled man.

They cruised over a hilly glade about a quarter of a mile from the cabin. It was a sunny, clear day with the temperature still staying a little below twenty degrees. The machines made crisscrossing track marks in the untouched snow and soon the long, parallel lines zigzagged over the surface like a giant web. The snowmobile motors buzzed through the afternoon, the noise breaking the otherwise still air. The men were almost ready to end their practice runs when they saw a Piper Cub aircraft drop in low over the treetops. The pilot dipped down over the men below and rocked his wings. Fuller waved to the man in the airplane.

"It's Coffin," he yelled to the others. "He's come."

* * *

Miles Coffin landed the small plane in a clearing near the lodge. He had been here before and knew how to handle the air currents for a perfect landing in the limited space. In the past, Coffin had been a guide on hunts for the partners, Fuller and Mason. The former owner of the lodge, an ex-army colonel who spent most of his retired days hosting wild hunting and drinking parties, had also paid for Coffin's services on occasion. The man had died after falling on his own rifle while intoxicated.

Coffin taxied the plane to the edge of the clearing, cut the engine and climbed out of the cabin. The snow was soft and he sank into the white powder a full six inches. It would be easy to run a wolf pack down in this, he thought. He lifted his rifle and shotgun out of the plane and placed them carefully on the packs which he dropped by his feet. He slipped his .45 automatic into a leather holster and strapped it around his waist. He was ready for the hunt.

A snowmobile rounded the edge of the pine trees on the rim of the airstrip. It was driven by Fuller. He was alone. As the machine drew closer Coffin greeted him.

"I see your party is here," Coffin said as Fuller pulled up beside him.

"Yep," Fuller said. "They arrived. A great bunch we got this time. Getting their jollies by gunning down wolves."

"I met them in Fairbanks," Coffin said. "Salt of the earth," he added sarcastically.

* * *

Coffin entered the cabin behind Fuller and hung his gear on the wall by the front door. The members of the hunting party were waiting at the bar.

"We meet again," Giff greeted Coffin, his voice thorny.

"Good evening, gentlemen," Coffin said, approaching them.

"What was all that bull you were giving us at the hotel in Fairbanks?" Giff said. "Were you conning us or just feeling us out?"

"I like to get a feel of who I take on a hunt."

"Did we pass inspection?" Giff spat the words at the hunter.

"If you feel my services are not required I will be moving on," Coffin said, directing his words at Giff.

Giff turned his back on Coffin and leaned over the bar. He would not commit himself to the lone position of severing the bond Fuller and Mason had made with Coffin, although he would like to call it quits right now. He saw Coffin only as trouble.

"Just hold on here," Max interrupted. "What seems to be the problem?"

"No problem, Max," Giff said. "Coffin and I just don't see eye to eye on a few things. That's all."

"Hell," Max said, "we can't be going on a hunt disagreeing with each other. We have to cooperate. Especially with our guides."

"It doesn't really matter," Giff said to Fuller. "I'll take your word on this, Fuller. If you think you need him then that suits me. You must have faith in him."

"Coffin is the man we prefer to be with us," Fuller said.

"This isn't going to work," Coffin said. "I shouldn't have come."

"Nonsense," Max said. "This is no way to start a relationship. I'm Max Taylor." Max held out his hand to Coffin. "I organized this hunt. If Fuller vouches for you that's good enough for me."

* * *

The men spent the rest of the evening sorting their equipment. Fuller and his partner cleaned and checked the shotguns which were to be used in the morning while their guests laid out heavier clothing. Giff took a holster from his grip and strapped it to his waist. He lifted a .44 Magnum Ruger Blackhawk revolver out of its sheath and hefted it in his hands.

"What's that for?" Coffin asked.

"That's just in case the wolves get too close," Giff said.

Just in case. Coffin thought of the words he had said to Lucy. He fell silent.

Giff sat down on a leather couch and loaded shells into the weapon. Coffin turned away from him and went to the bar where he poured himself a scotch.

Andy watched the two men. He could feel the tension between them like a tangible substance. He wondered just what it would take for Giff's obvious dislike of Coffin to erupt into the violence he knew his brother was capable of. He had spoken little to Giff since they had left New York, knowing his own relationship with him was always strained. Since their first confrontation Giff and Miles Coffin labored through what appeared to be a forced, tense atmosphere. Giff was volatile, ready to burst. It was obvious to Andy and he felt that Max sensed it also.

"How many wolves do you figure we might get?" Max asked Coffin.

Coffin sipped his drink and hung an elbow on the bar. When no one answered he realized that the question had been tossed at him.

"It's hard to say," he answered. "If we're lucky and the weather holds we could have a good hunt."

"There's no limit in this area," Giff interjected. "We can kill as many as we want."

"How many do you intend to kill?" Coffin asked.

"Well, there are three of us," Giff said icily. "We ought to go back with at least one kill each."

"It's possible, but unpredictable," Coffin said. "If we catch a pack in the open right off, we stand a chance of getting a few; that is if we can stop them from getting to the protection of the under-growth. But, even then, taking more than two or three at one time is impractical. The carcasses have to be cleaned and moved. It's better to take as few as possible on each outing."

"Is that your advice or are you telling us what to do?" Giff said.

"You're paying me to keep things right," Coffin snapped back.

"It's not your function to limit a hunt," Giff said, obviously irritated. "You just take us where we want to go."

"Let me ask you a question," Coffin said. "How long do you plan on staying?"

"As long as it takes to get what we want," Giff answered.

"Our deal was for twelve days, maximum," Fuller said. "We have other commitments after that."

"There's the outside chance we may not trap a pack at all during the time we are here," Coffin said. "There is no guarantee that we will kill even one wolf. It isn't as easy to take them on the ground as you may think. You've got to find them first. You can't call ahead for a reservation."

Giff grunted. "We'd better trap a pack. That's what we're paying for. And you guys are the experts. You take our money and we expect to shoot wolves."

"But Coffin is right," Fuller said. "There is no guarantee. You must realize that. Certainly you have hunted before and came away with nothing."

"Let's knock off this bickering," Max interrupted. "It's getting us nowhere. I'm not going to quibble over a few bucks. I made a deal and I'll accept the outcome."

It quieted Giff down for a moment.

Then he said to Fuller "You want us to use snowmobiles. I'd prefer to shoot from a plane. But you say it's against the law. I'd be willing to make it worth your while to let us use that plane Coffin came in on. I expect to leave here with a couple of good wolf skins, no matter what it takes."

"Out of the question," Coffin said. "My plane stays on the ground."

"Name your price," Giff insisted.

"Go to hell," Coffin swore.

"We'll do our best, Mr. Taylor," Fuller said, slightly flustered. "We get good results from snowmobiles. We have two spike cabins about ten miles north of here. We keep gasoline and supplies there. We'll use the cabins as our base. We can cover a large area. We'll cross these and the new snow should help us tremendously."

"How many wolves in a pack?" Andy asked, attempting to ease the tension by changing the subject.

"They vary," Coffin answered. "I've known a pack to have as few as six and as many as thirty. It's difficult to say."

"Do you know the packs in the area where we'll hunt?"

"Circumstances change the conditions by which a pack will remain in a territory," Coffin said. "A severe winter. Lack of game. They sometimes move to find food. Sometimes too many die off over a bad winter and the pack will roam. They follow the caribou herds for hundreds of miles."

"When was the last hunt you had up here?" Max joined in the questioning.

"A wolf hunt?" Fuller asked.

"Yes," Max said.

"We haven't hunted wolves since last November," Fuller said. "And that was a predator control trip. But what difference does that make?"

"Things may have changed since then," Max suggested. "Maybe the wolves aren't where we're going."

"We've scouted the territories and I've seen packs," Fuller said. "I don't foresee any bad luck."

"When do we start?" Andy asked.

"Before dawn," Fuller replied.

CHAPTER 17

In the morning the men gathered into three groups and set out for the spike cabins to the north. Giff rode behind Fuller on the lead machine while Andy doubled with Coffin on the second. Max and Willie Mason brought up the rear.

The temperature still held at just under twenty degrees as the three machines cut sharp grooves into the undisturbed snow beyond the edge of the surrounding forest. The dawn was breaking in a cloud-spotted sky. The rays of the sun tinted the cloud edges with a glowing peach color. Hoarfrost sparkled everywhere like jewels in the approaching sunlight.

Soon the spring would come, ending the long, dark nights. The days would grow longer and, by summer, the sunlight would outlast the dark.

The efficient machines buzzed over the white terrain like giant metallic bugs, kicking up sprays of misty snow. They moved quickly, clipping along at a pace of over thirty miles per hour.

Andy sat behind Coffin, the fur-lined hood of his jacket pulled over his head and snapped tight around his neck. His gloved hands cradled the unloaded pump-action shotgun in his lap. He had not loaded the gun. The shells were in his pockets.

The man guiding the machine puzzled Andy. He was a living contradiction. He professed an unnatural interest, almost protective of the animal they hunted, and yet he had killed them by the hundreds. Andy wanted to talk to Coffin. He wanted to know why the man who preached the nobility of the wolf served as a commercial guide to run the animal down and kill him.

Within hours, the small procession came in sight of the two small spike cabins. They lay in a ravine at the base of a series of snow-covered ridges. It seemed to Andy the most unlikely place to have situated the cabins. They seemed vulnerable, overwhelmed by the bulk of the terrain which enclosed them. On either side they were completely surrounded by dense pine trees. Only in the direction from which the men entered was there immediate access to the two cabins.

Andy realized his judgement was wrong when Coffin spoke to him.

"The cabins are protected on three sides," he said. "The woods cut down the winds and shield the cabins somewhat during storms."

The men assembled before the small cabins and left the machines. Fuller led them inside the first building. When they gathered around him he explained the situation.

"We have food and supplies here. In each of the cabins. We store a supply of fuel for the machines and sufficient ammunition to last us through any hunt. As you can see there are bunk beds. We will spend a few days at these cabins. There is plenty of wood. We'll split up into two groups. One group in each cabin."

"When do we go back to the lodge?" Max asked.

"Not for a few days or unless it becomes necessary," Fuller replied. "We'll be traveling a great deal each day, covering a lot of territory. That is, unless we get lucky right away."

Andy noticed that the small cabin was almost a scaled-down duplicate of the lodge they had just left except that it contained no bar, kitchen, or upper sleeping loft. It was built of hewn logs, laid one upon the other. A stone fireplace was the center point of the structure. A pile of cut logs lay on the stone hearth.

"We're going about twenty miles farther north for the hunt," Fuller said. "We'll take time to top off our fuel. If anyone is hungry, now is the time to grab a bite. We'll leave in about half an hour."

Andy drifted closer to Max. When he was standing within earshot he spoke softly to him. "How are you doing, Max? Feeling all right?"

"I'm fine," Max was quick to answer. But he couldn't hide the expression that Andy saw in his face. It was as if Max were tortured by a prodding problem that would not go away. He seemed to be fighting some kind of battle within himself that was now obvious only to those who looked for its effects. Max was sick and in some pain. He could no longer hide it. Andy felt sure. Something was wrong with him and this trip was taking a toll on him.

"How are you and Coffin getting along?" Max asked, changing the subject.

"Okay," Andy replied. "He doesn't say much."

"I think it's a good idea if you kept him out of Giff's way," Max said. "They don't get along."

"I'll stay with him," Andy said.

The men were making steaks on a grill near the fireplace. The smell of the cooking meat filled the confined quarters.

"We won't eat again until late in the day," Fuller said. "So let's fill up."

*   *   *

For two days the men patrolled the area adjacent to their home base. They covered hundreds of square miles, zigzagging back across their own paths many times. Because the snowmobiles did not navigate as well in densely wooded areas they were forced to stay in the open. Coffin led the party on the trail of a wolf pack on three separate occasions, but in each instance, the tracks they followed took them to the edge of a forest where the wolves had vanished into the thicket.

Only once did they actually encounter wolves. On the second day out they witnessed a pack venturing out of the cover of the woodland. But the men were too far away and by the time they gave chase the wolves had already vanished from sight.

The men were getting frustrated and it was rapidly beginning to show, especially on Giff, who took to grumbling.

"What the hell is wrong?" Giff asked Fuller at the end of the second day. "How come we're not making contact with any wolves? I thought your guy Coffin had all the answers."

"They're afraid of us," Fuller said. "They've taken to the woods to avoid us."

"Isn't that the way it always is?" Giff said. "That's nothing new to you wolf hunters. You should know how to flush them into the open."

"Don't worry," Fuller reassured him. "The wolves have got to eat. They have to hunt. They will come out of the woods to hunt. That's when we'll get them."

*　*　*

Coffin took the lead again when they resumed their journey on the third day. The small caravan pushed north over the snow, leaving tracks once again in long intercepting lines. In the span of a few hours they had once again crossed into the territorial boundaries laid down by Midnight's pack.

There was hardly any wind and the sun was bright in the cloudless sky. Although the temperature was well below the freezing mark it still did not feel overly cold. The sun was melting some of the snow that clung to clumps of ice.

"This is great weather," Coffin said without preamble or turning his head to look back at Andy. "We couldn't ask for a better day."

"Isn't it a little mild for Alaska?" Andy asked. "I thought it was bitterly cold up here all the time."

"This time of the year it isn't too bad," Coffin answered. "It can still get pretty rough though. Much too cold to hunt up here in the winter months."

"That's what Jim Fuller said."

"Even the animals have it tough," Coffin said. "More than half the young don't make it through their first winter. The wolf packs attack the young and the weak. What the wolves don't get the cold does. And the wolves lose many of their own in battles with large game, to disease or starvation."

"It balances itself out," Andy said.

"Yeah. And man balances it in his favor."

In his few conversations with Miles Coffin so far Andy learned that the man would bluntly say what was on his mind. Regardless that he was hired by men from a far different world than his, he freely showed his displeasure of their motives.

"You don't much care for hunters," Andy said flatly, taking the lead from Coffin.

"But I am a hunter," Coffin answered. "I'm not against the man who has a sane purpose."

"Our kind of hunter, I mean. The big city guy with plenty of money who calls it sport."

"You mean Giff?"

"Not him specifically."

"I don't care for the motives," Coffin said. "They've made it into a game rather than a sport. Does it bother you that I feel this way?"

"No. Not me. I have no convictions about the honor or integrity of hunting. The others would give you an argument though."

Coffin was silent a moment. Then he said "What do you do for a living?"

"I paint. I'm an artist."

"Interesting," Coffin said. "What subject matter?"

"It varies. I'm not an abstract painter. My stuff is very realistic. It runs the gamut, a broad view of the working man in America."

"Is your stuff good?"

"That's difficult for me to answer. Sometimes I think it is. And there are times when I want to burn everything."

Coffin fell silent again. He didn't speak for a long while. Then suddenly he pointed to a spot on the crest of a snow-capped ridge. "See there," he said.

"What is it?" Andy asked.

"Ravens," Coffin said. "See them? The flock of big black birds. There."

"Yes," Andy said. "What about them?"

"They will lead us to the wolves," Coffin said.

CHAPTER 18

When Coffin's plane arrived, roaring over the treetops and disappearing behind them, the wolves became disoriented. Of the members of the pack, only Midnight associated the plane with the environment of man in which he had lived. He knew the coming of man meant destruction and death for the wolves.

Because he was a strong, fierce animal, Midnight had survived the ravages of hunger, blizzards, the threats of wolf packs and even savage fights with large game he attacked alone. It had taken every moment he lived in the wild to learn how to survive. Now, as the undaunted leader of a wolf pack, he would not allow man to capture or hurt him. He would not be penned or chained as he had once been. He would die first.

The pack followed Midnight as he left the deep snow and moved into a nearby woodland. Here the snow was older and more firmly packed. The wolves were able to negotiate better under the covering of the trees. With the coming of spring the deep snow would soon melt and hunting would become a simpler task. Now, it was extremely difficult to move in the deep, granular snowfall.

Midnight led the pack back to their lair. They had dug out

some of the food still buried in their frozen storehouse caches. They had to dig through many inches of loosening ice and snow before they unearthed the precious meat. But this supply wouldn't sustain the wolves for long. The never-ending pangs of hunger would not let them rest.

The pack hunted throughout the night. Midnight slept during the day in short sessions, never deeply, his naps constantly interrupted by a sense of activity around him. At night he took out a small party consisting of his eldest male offspring and three subordinate hunters. Moon and the rest of the pack remained behind near the site of the lair.

The small band set off into the crisp night that had turned much colder once the sun had set. A thin crust of ice quickly formed on the surface of the snow. It was not thick enough to hold the weight of the wolves' bodies and it crunched under them as they moved. There would be no easy kill tonight. If they were lucky enough to come upon game they would not be able to run it down. Practically any long-legged creature would escape in the difficult terrain.

After a long, tiring search Midnight returned with the four wolves trailing behind. They were tired and hungry, having found no game all night. They labored, climbing the hill to where the pack rested and dropped quickly into a restful sleep. That night they had traveled many difficult miles in circling patterns that crossed and recrossed their own tracks. All to no avail. In the morning they would once again venture forth with the entire pack to seek the elusive prey they so direly needed. All the members were severely hungry and needed more than the meager morsels from the winter storehouses and the small game they had been living on lately.

But the winter was ending soon. The anticipation of easier days and nights of hunting lifted the pack's spirits. The great snows would melt and the caribou would return to feed in the meadows and glades. The wolves had only to make it through the next month or so when the brief spring would inevitably come and their food supply would increase.

* * *

Midnight slept for a few hours and set off with the entire pack before the dawn broke. He led them through the deep snow, keeping always to the edge of the woods. They headed south, away from the direction he had hunted during the night. It would be hours before they had maneuvered themselves downwind of any game. They were seeking a position that would give them advantage over their prey. The pack trudged across a meadow, leaving a deep rut carved in the untouched surface. Midnight, as always, was in the lead position and the pack followed behind him in a long single file.

Ahead, high in the sky, a flock of ever-present ravens urged the wolf pack onward. They too had been hungry lately. The wolf pack had not had a major kill in a long while and the big black birds were in a similar plight. They would perform well, working hand-in-hand with the pack as they had so many times in the past. The wolves plodded on, slowly making their way through the difficult terrain, following the lead of the birds upon whom they now completely relied. The wind held steadily from the north and, after hours on the journey, they had not been able to pick up the scent of any game. On the rise of a hill the pack watched the birds change direction and disappear over a ridge of pine trees. When the pack finally sighted the black birds they had rounded a wooded grove and were heading north. The wolves followed them slowly into a small, steep valley.

The scent of caribou reached the sensitive nostrils of the wolves and the smell spurred them onwards with an intensity nurtured by their hunger. They were well into the floor of the valley when they heard a droning sound that broke the silent air. It was a strange noise, something that confused the wolves and stopped them short in their tracks. The sound came from behind them and its soft roar was drawing closer. The frightened pack circled around Midnight not knowing what was happening to them.

CHAPTER 19

The ravens vanished behind the rise of a pine-spotted hill. Coffin pressed the group onward, much like the leader of a wolf pack. He turned and signaled to Fuller who followed close behind him. Coffin pointed to where the birds had gone. Fuller nodded ascent. The snowmobile gathered speed and topped the summit of the hill. At the peak, Coffin slowed the machine until the others caught up to him.

"There are your wolves," Coffin said to Andy, indicating the circling pack below on the valley floor. "We're lucky. We caught them perfectly. Conditions couldn't be better for us or worse for them."

The other machines drew alongside Coffin. Andy heard Giff cry out. "God damn! Look at that big black one leading them. Let's get them."

All the men were talking and gaping in wonder at their first sight of a wolf pack. It was like watching fantasy manifest into reality.

"I've never seen anything so marvelous," Andy said spontaneously.

Coffin turned abruptly and looked into Andy's eyes. He smiled at his passenger.

"Come on," Giff yelled to them. "We're wasting time."

Coffin adjusted his sunglasses. He pulled them down to the tip of his nose. He had to be certain. The large black wolf out there could be Midnight, he thought. Coffin squinted his eyes. It was Midnight! He was sure certain. The hatred stirred in him. Visions of Lucy's mutilated corpse flooded his mind. An overwhelming desire to kill the wolf raged within him. By now the pursuit of the black wolf had become an obsession, like Ahab and his white whale.

It was over a year since Coffin had lost Midnight's trail. The fruitless months he had spent in the interior indiscriminately killing wolves had hardened him to their plight. He no longer cared how or why they died. After Lucy's terrible death he saw wolves only as symbols of her death.

"Let's get going!" Giff cried.

"Hold on," Coffin said. "We do this right. We spread out and flank them. Keep far enough apart so that we won't end up shooting each other. Mason will bring up the rear. We'll keep the pack ahead of us and pinned down on the flanks. If they try to get away to the rear they'll be trapped."

"Sounds good," Giff said. "Can't proceed without a game plan."

Below, in the valley, the wolves had assembled behind the large black wolf who was obviously the leader. Andy glared in fascination as the pack began to move up the valley. The lead wolf crashed through the snow. The others quickly fell in behind him. A pure white wolf, as flawless as the snow around it, followed directly to the rear of the black leader.

God, Andy thought, what was he doing here with a shotgun in his hands, about to kill these magnificent animals? To what purpose? What gives him the right? They belong here. He certainly didn't.

Coffin raised his arm and motioned for the group to move forward. The machines sprang into action, churning up chunks of snow as they sped down the hill. The snowmobiles functioned perfectly in the environment for which they were made and were soon closing the distance between them and the wolves. The pack plodded desperately through the deep snow, terrified by the unknown threat that pursued them. Midnight pushed forward, fearing for the pack. He changed his direction and angled towards the dense woods to the east. The wolves would be safer there and able to move quicker in the thinner layer of snow.

Coffin saw that Midnight had made a subtle turn so he signaled to Fuller to make the adjustment. It was definitely Midnight, Coffin realized. No doubt about it. He was a smart wolf. If the pack made it into the woods the men would not follow them in. They would have to give up pursuing the wolves. There was no way they would be able to give chase in the thick woods.

It soon became obvious, as the distance between the wolves and the hunters closed, that the wolf pack could not outrun the snowmobiles. The maneuverability of the machines on the frozen surface was much greater than that of the pack. As the men caught up to the wolves the safety of the woods became impossibly far. The frightened animals became erratic and sprinted in different directions.

Coffin signaled for Fuller to close on the right flank. They were getting very close to a struggling wolf who was at the very end of the pack. He was the first wolf to be overtaken. He was an omega animal whose position was last.

"Load up," Coffin said to Andy.

Andy took a handful of shells from his jacket pocket and slipped them into the pump-action shotgun.

"We're coming up on this wolf," Coffin said over the roar of the motor. "Do you want to take him?"

"No," Andy said evenly.

Coffin nodded. He turned to Fuller and signaled once again. He pointed at the wolf closest to him, gesturing that Fuller close in and take the wolf out. Andy could see Giff bring his shotgun to his shoulder and take aim. Coffin slowed his machine slightly so that he fell back, out of the line of fire. Fuller's machine drew closer to the helpless wolf who was floundering in the deep snow. The distance to the animal was so close that Andy could see his tongue hanging from his mouth, his ragged breathing forming heavy vapor in the cold morning air. What a place to be, he thought. How many men ever get to witness what was happening here this morning?

The snowmobile on which Giff was riding dipped into a depression in the snow and dropped suddenly just as he opened fire. The sudden bump jolted Giff and the sound exploded in the valley, the shot flying harmlessly over the wolf. Andy heard Giff yell at Fuller to hold the machine steady. When he fired the second shot it did not miss the mark. It ripped through the wolf, killing him instantly and driving his broken body into the snow.

Giff raised the Mossberg shotgun over his head and shouted, "Yahoo! Ride 'em down!"

Coffin steered the snowmobile closer to the fallen wolf.

"Get ready," Coffin told Andy. "Just in case he's not dead."

Andy raised the shotgun as Coffin slowed the machine. When they drew close to the fallen animal it was obvious that he was dead. The shot had torn away part of the animal's head and shoulder. Spots of blood stained the trampled snow where the wolf had gone down. Coffin raised his hand to signal Fuller.

"Dead," Coffin yelled.

"Let's get the rest of them," Giff cried out. "Speed up. Come on!"

Fuller responded and the machine pulled ahead. Coffin gunned his snowmobile and shot back into formation. Behind them the third machine slowed to view the fallen wolf. Andy heard Max shout "Son-of-a-bitch!"

Andy cradled the shotgun in his lap and held on as the machine picked up speed. Ahead, the wolves had put some distance between themselves and the men who pursued them. But the swiftness of the snowmobiles again quickly closed the gap and, within minutes, they had overtaken the trailing members of the wolf pack.

Andy watched as Giff again took aim. A burst dropped the wolf closest to him. The animal stumbled and fell. As he lay wounded in the snow his legs kept churning instinctively in a running motion.

Coffin pulled in close to the wolf and brought the snowmobile to a stop. Andy automatically raised his gun to a ready position. Fuller pulled up beside them.

"God damn!" Giff shouted. "I got him. Look at his legs go. He thinks he's still running."

Coffin reached inside his sheepskin jacket and produced his .45 automatic. He cocked the gun and aimed it at the wolf. A single shot to the heart stopped the animal's motion.

"Nice shot," Giff said, grinning.

Coffin turned away from the wolf and pointed to the fleeing pack. "Follow me," he instructed Fuller and the rest of the party.

Coffin spurred the machine into action. He held the .45 in his right hand while he steered with the left. The other snowmobiles raced along behind him. Soon they again closed the distance to the wolves. But the panicky members of the pack were nearing the entrance to the dense woods and safety.

Coffin pulled well ahead of the other machines and was drawing within yards of the running animals. Andy suddenly feared for his own life. What if the wolves turned on them? There were no more than a dozen altogether, but their size and motion in the snow disturbed him. He had never been in a life and death struggle with wild animals and he found it extremely difficult to control his emotions. He wondered if any of the others felt the same fear he did. He doubted it. They were all experienced hunters. The guides had certainly been in countless situations like this. Giff and Max were probably excited by the encounter. Andy felt cowardly and ashamed. He realized that he had a loaded shotgun in his hands and could easily protect himself if he had to. The odds were in his favor and against the wolves.

The snowmobile glided up behind the trailing members of the struggling pack. Coffin lifted the .45 and aimed it at the nearest wolf. He fired point blank. His shot took the wolf in the right side and pummeled him to the ground. Coffin slowed the machine to a halt.

The other two machines had caught up. Coffin waved Fuller down. "Let them go," he said. "We'll get them tomorrow or another time."

"What the hell is going on?" Giff shouted. "Why don't we get the rest of the wolves? They're getting away."

"That's all for the day," Coffin said.

"Bullshit," Giff swore. "What the hell are you doing? We're getting after those wolves. Now!"

Coffin ignored Giff and stepped off the machine. He walked to the dead animal. He slipped a hunting knife from its sheath and dug it into the wolf's underbelly. He sliced a long cut down the flesh and began to methodically remove the pelt.

"What the fuck!" Giff swore, jumping from the machine he was riding. "Who the hell do you think you are, Coffin? Shooting our wolves and then stopping when you feel like. You were hired as a fucking guide. That's all."

Coffin stood up from his task and stared at Giff.

"We've got more wolves than we can handle right now," he said. "There's plenty of time to shoot more."

"Like hell!" Giff cried. "Look up there." He pointed to the escaping wolves. "They're getting away. We may never have a chance like this again."

"Let it go," Coffin said calmly. "You're pushing it."

Giff could no longer contain his anger and frustration. He suddenly lashed out at Coffin with a fierce blow that, had it landed, would surely have flattened him. But the tall man saw the shot come and sidestepped. He brought his right arm up quickly and caught the blow on his shoulder. He turned and faced Giff squarely, both fists cocked.

"Come on. Help yourself," he challenged Giff.

They faced each other. Giff moved in closer, circling Coffin. He feigned with a few left jabs, feeling Coffin out. The taller man again caught them on his arm. Suddenly Giff moved swiftly, his acumen and experience at boxing showing. Two quick blows caught Coffin and knocked him off balance.

"Damn it!" Andy yelled at them. "Stop it!"

Coffin realized Giff was serious and out to prove his manhood. He raised his hands to protect himself. Giff struck again, just as quickly. This time he caught Coffin on the temple and knocked him to his knees.

Behind them Max left the machine he was on and trounced through the snow to where the two men confronted each other.

Giff closed in as Coffin got to his feet in the snow. He was off balance but he caught Giff's left arm in an arm lock and struck a fierce blow to Giff's stomach. Giff doubled over, coughing. Coffin could have finished it right there as Giff slipped to the snow. He cocked his right arm to hit Giff in the face. He held it poised.

"What the hell is going on here?" Max exclaimed, as he came alongside the two struggling men.

Giff got to his feet slowly and fought for breath.

"Our guide here is calling off the hunt for today," Giff managed.

"Why?" Max demanded.

"Mr. Taylor," Fuller interjected. "We have to skin the wolves we killed. We can't continue until we clean up here. We have plenty of time to pick up the hunt."

"Crap," Giff said. "This situation is perfect. I want that big black wolf. And we're just killing valuable time here arguing with this guy."

"Take it easy, Giff," Max said. "Maybe Fuller is right. This is their show, after all."

Coffin continued the task he had begun. He calmly and methodically skinned the dead wolf.

"Damn it, Max," Giff swore. "This guy's done as much killing as we did today. Suppose we don't have another opportunity like this. Suppose we don't catch another pack under such ideal conditions?"

"What about that, Fuller?" Max asked.

"Highly unlikely," Fuller said. "We still have plenty of time. We are now in this particular pack's territory. We'll be able to track them down."

"It's too late today anyhow," Andy said. He gestured to the wolf pack. The men turned to see where Andy was pointing. Five hundred yards up the slope of the valley the black leader had made it to the shelter of the trees and the wolves were following him into the thick woods.

"Kiss them off now," Giff cursed.

Coffin resumed his task. When he was finished he lifted the skin clear of the wolf's carcass and dragged it to the snowmobile, leaving a bloody trail in the snow. He deposited the pelt beside the machine Giff had been riding.

"How big is that wolf?" Giff asked Fuller.

"I'd guess about eighty or ninety pounds."

"How big would you say the black leader is?" Giff asked.

"What difference does it make?" Andy said.

"Because that's the one I want," Giff said. "That's the one I came here to get. He's a lot bigger than this one. I said I'd settle for one good trophy. And I'm not leaving without him."

Coffin frowned. He turned to Fuller. "Let's skin the rest of the dead wolves," he murmured.

CHAPTER 20

The men had come back into Midnight's life. They had come with their noise and their booming, sudden death. They caught the pack in a precarious situation and had taken advantage of their vulnerability.

The ear-shattering noise made by the men had dropped three of the subordinate wolves who trailed at the end of the pack. Midnight felt the imminent danger and he urged the remainder of the pack onward to safety. Moon stayed directly behind him and his two remaining offspring behind her.

Midnight forced his weight through the burdensome soft snow, cleaving a trail in which the pack followed. By tramping down the snow he made it easier for the smaller wolves to move. The lesser wolves were frightened and on the verge of panic. They had never before experienced death from man, so quick and loud. Only the persistence of their large leader directing them to the woods kept them from erratic action.

The men's machines no longer made the droning sound after the sharp, crashing noises which killed the wolves. The men did not pursue the pack. They had stopped and were taking the pelts of the wolves they had killed.

Midnight pushed harder, straining the muscles of his tired body to extraordinary effort. He and his wolf pack were hungry, still not having a good kill in weeks. The small game they had been living off recently did not give them the energy needed to conduct one good hunt, let alone stand up to the exertion to which their bodies had been pushed today.

Unrelenting, Midnight crashed through the final snow barrier and broke into the shelter of a grove of dense spruce. The lighter snowfall inside the woods made the going suddenly easier. The other wolves scampered in after him. He led them deeper into the shade of the thicket until, finally, they were able to stop and relax.

Down in the valley the machines moved away from the direction the pack had gone. The wind had changed, and, filtered through the woodland, Midnight picked up the scent of the men. It mingled on the clear air along with the smell of the freshly killed wolves. The smell was intoxicating. The pack would survive. They would eat tonight.

* * *

Colder air came once again with the setting sun. The night was blue in the light of the full moon as Midnight cautiously brought the pack down to the floor of the valley where their brethren lay dead. They stayed close to the perimeter of the woods, remembering that the death noise from the men struck quickly and from a distance. If it became necessary they could jump back into the woods and be lost in a minute.

They detected no sight or smell of man. Only the scent of the exposed flesh of the dead wolves lingered on the slight wind. Midnight left the woodland edge and slowly descended the sloping valley wall. The pack followed in a single file. When he arrived at the carcasses the ravens and other predators had already eaten some of the dead bodies. The wolves gathered around the body of the first dead wolf and waited while their leader ate its flesh. When he finished, the others joined in the meal. Half the pack had moved off with Moon to the body of the second wolf and quickly fell to the task of devouring what remained of that carcass.

After they had eaten the flesh of the fallen wolves the pack gathered around Midnight. He started off in a northerly direction, away from the route the men had traveled, north to where the herds wandered in the no-man's land between the neighboring pack territories, away from the danger of the men who had come to end their lives.

* * *

Coffin and the two guides hung the wolf pelts outside the spike cabin on a west wall. They had skinned the animals with great expertise, stripping each entire body of pelts, including the head and the left front leg, which was required to remain for sealing by the Game and Fish Department. Giff stood in the snow outside the cabin, Max by his side.

"Not like the one in Fairbanks," Giff said.

"No," Max responded. "But, what the hell. We didn't come here to break any records. We came to hunt wolves and that's what we're doing."

"Damn it, Max," Giff said. "Did you see that big black wolf?"

"How could I miss him?"

"I'm not going back without him," Giff vowed.

"Giff," Max said calmly, "you might as well face it. That pack is hell and gone. The chances of finding that same pack of wolves when we go back out are pretty slim, no matter what Fuller says."

"It's that damn Coffin," Giff swore. "It's his fault. What the hell kind of an outfit is this? He was shooting as much as we were today. He actually gunned down one of the wolves. The guys who run this hunt are taking orders from him, like he was some kind of god. He stopped me from getting that wolf."

"Why don't you forget that black wolf?" Max said.

"Forget him? You've got to be kidding, Max. You know what it feels like to get that great a kill. There aren't that many in a guy's life. The truly great ones. Those few are special. That black wolf is one of those few. He's special. And I mean for him to be my kill. Not yours. Not Coffin's. Mine."

"These men know what they're doing," Max said. "We don't want anything to go wrong."

"Nothing's going to go wrong," Giff said. "We're paying for this trip. We have a right to make demands."

"There isn't a hell of a lot more we can demand that we haven't already."

Giff was smoking a cigarette as he spoke to Max. The smoke formed white clouds around his head as he puffed furiously. He shot the butt off the ends of his fingers and it struck one of the wolf pelts in a shower of sparks.

"We'll see," he said angrily.

*   *   *

The men split into two groups. Max, Giff and Andy in one cabin; Coffin, Fuller and Mason in the other. The night still came early in the late winter, leaving daylight as the shortest phase.

Max lit two kerosene lamps provided by Fuller and set them on either side of the interior of the cabin. Andy and Giff brought in logs from the supply shed situated between the two cabins and soon they had a fire blazing. The heat from the stone fireplace filled the cabin immediately.

Max was busy making a meal of steaks and potatoes on the wood-burning stove. There was no running water and no electricity. Water had been brought with them from the lodge in insulated canisters. There was room for only one table and a few wooden chairs along with bunks in each cabin. The men took turns eating their meals.

When they finished eating Giff opened a bottle of Jack Daniels and passed it around the room. Andy got glasses from a cabinet and handed one to each man.

"Well, drink up," Max said. "Our first wolf hunt."

The three men raised their glasses and drank. While Max and Giff saluted with fervor Andy raised his reluctantly.

"Three wolves," Max said. "Not bad."

"Damn it, Max," Giff swore. "We only shot two. That bastard Coffin killed the other one."

"What's the difference?" Andy said.

"It's our hunt," Giff snapped. "He's nothing but a damned guide. I don't know what his problem is but he deliberately let that black wolf get away."

Giff paused a moment, his eyes focusing on the wavering flames in the fireplace. His eyes glazed with a vision only he saw.

"I'll tell you one thing," he said. "If that bastard Coffin gets in the way again he's going to get fired. I'm letting you know so you better expect it."

"All right, Giff," Max said. "But let Fuller have a go at it first. If things don't work out to our liking then we'll do something about it."

"We don't need Coffin," Giff insisted. "All he did so far was interfere. I could have taken that whole pack out by myself."

"Come on, Giff," Andy said. "Coffin is here for a purpose. Fuller and Mason are experienced hunters. They wouldn't bring someone like Coffin along if they didn't have faith in his ability. We got what we wanted today. Coffin did what he thought best. Look how much trouble it was bringing back those three wolf skins. How many wolves could we have brought back on one trip anyhow?"

Giff's stare ripped into Andy's eyes. Max suddenly saw, in the intensity of Giff's leer, a rift between his sons he had not seen before. Giff had never shown such anger towards his younger brother as Max now saw in his expression.

"Fuck you, Andy!" Giff swore, his voice edged with malice. "You taking sides?"

"No," Andy said. "But remember, Coffin is in his environment. He knows what he's doing. We don't."

"Son of a bitch!" Giff cried. "If this isn't a damn joke. Listen to who's telling me about hunting. When the hell did you decide you know more about hunting than anyone else in this room? The one time you shot something you threw up like a girl."

"Giff!" Max cried out.

"Hell, Max," Giff defended himself. "It's true and you know it. Sure, he went along with us. Like now. But he was always too good for us. He just tolerates us."

"That's enough, Giff!" Max said angrily.

"But he was never too proud to take your money," Giff continued.

"What the hell is this?" Max swore. "What's going on between you two?"

Andy turned away from Giff and sat down on a lower bunk. He dropped his head as if the action might remove him from the scene which was ensuing. He did not mean to start an argument by defending Coffin. He should have realized Giff was ready to explode because the black wolf, the target of his desire on this hunt, had escaped. And he had offered himself as the alternate target for Giff's inevitable venom.

"I'm sick of this fucking kid!" Giff cried. "Begging him to come into the business. Begging him to go hunting with us. He doesn't belong. He never did. He shouldn't even be a part of our family."

"Damn it, Giff," Max said. "What's wrong with you? Why are you acting like this?"

Andy lifted his head. He looked directly into Max's eyes. The pained look had returned to his father's face.

"We just don't agree about Coffin's authority," Andy said. "That's all, Max. Giff is angry because the black wolf got away."

"Fuck you, Andy!" Giff cried. His anger had peaked. "You don't belong here, you goddamn leech."

"Giff!" Max shouted. "You're acting like a spoiled kid. Cut it out! What's eating you?"

"I'm acting like a kid?" Giff was incredulous. "That's funny coming from you, Max. What the hell were you acting like when you bought every one of Andy's paintings from the gallery owner.

All along he thought he was good. Thought his junk was actually selling."

The words fell like a thunderclap in the small room. Max was stunned. How did Giff know? His face registered the shock as his mouth dropped open. He groped for the right words.

Andy was equally shocked. His astonishment quickly turned to anguish and a look of complete distress came over his face like a veil.

"Max!" he moaned. "You've been buying my paintings? You?"

Max couldn't have been more hurt if Giff had fired a bullet into his heart. He looked into Andy's eyes, searching for forgiveness.

"I'm sorry, son," he offered. "I couldn't help myself."

"Why?" It was all Andy could think of to say.

"I wanted you to be successful," Max stammered, trying to sound sincere. "You wouldn't let me help you by coming into the business. I always thought that if you wanted to paint you could do it in your spare time. But you wanted to paint and nothing else would satisfy you. I'm resigned to that. I didn't know how else to help you except buy your work."

"But now those sales are meaningless, Max," Andy said. "Can't you see that? Couldn't you leave me alone and let me make it on my own. When I became established you could make a legitimate purchase. You must know how important this is to me."

"I didn't understand," Max said, his eyes clouding with tears. "I'm sorry, Andy." He turned and faced Giff, his anger apparent in his strained words. "You didn't have to do this. There was no reason," he said, sorrowfully.

Giff did not respond. He turned away and would not look directly at Max.

Andy, by now, was simmering. He was glaring at Giff. His eyes narrowed to slits. He got up from the bunk and faced his brother.

"You miserable bastard," Andy swore. "You never did have any integrity."

Giff laughed short, derisive laughs.

"I'm not the bastard, Andy," he quipped. "Remember? You have the distinction of bearing that title."

"Damn you!" Andy cried. He leaped at Giff, both hands locking around his brother's throat. Andy drove Giff back against the cabin wall. A chair crashed to the floor as Max moved to separate his sons.

Giff broke Andy's grip and drove his right fist into his face. The blow caught Andy on his right cheekbone and knocked him back against the bunk. Andy shook the cobwebs from his head, raised his fists and charged Giff.

Max got between the two men and faced Giff. With a sudden quick motion he slapped Giff across the face with the open palm of his left hand. The sharp slap rang out like a pistol shot. It was an insulting blow to have come from his father; like chastising a naughty child. Not the way to treat a grown man. Giff grabbed his jacket from the bed and charged out of the cabin.

"I've never seen him like this," Max said. "I don't understand him at all."

CHAPTER 21

In the morning the men mounted the snowmobiles and set off after the wolves. Coffin, like his counterpart Midnight, led the party back to the site of the kill where they had left the stripped carcasses in the snow.

The dawn had not yet broken. In the dim, hazy light of morning the men gathered around the skeletal remains of the dead wolves.

"Who did this?" Giff asked.

Coffin pointed to the sets of tracks that converged on the spot where they had gathered.

"Wolves?" Giff asked. "You mean they ate their own kind?"

"That's right," Coffin answered. "They must not have had a large kill for awhile."

"Goddamn," Giff shuddered. "Gives you the creeps."

"See the tracks," Coffin said. "They all lead to a single file going away to the north. The wolves have carved a trail for us to follow."

"That's right!" Giff exclaimed. "Great."

Andy was again mounted behind Coffin on the lead snowmobile and Giff rode with Fuller. Max doubled up with Mason. Giff had avoided Andy since they started out. When their eyes did make contact Giff immediately turned away. The machines rolled over the snow with far greater speed than the wolf pack had been able to maintain. They kept to either side of the winding column of tracks made by the wolves. They had given the hunters a direct link to their whereabouts in the untrampled snow. A meeting was inevitable unless the pack changed course and had hidden somewhere in the thick woods along the route.

The wolves didn't stand a chance against the men and the machines, Andy thought. No wonder they had been slaughtered over the years. How can animals match the power and speed of snowmobiles, jeeps or planes? How can they stand up to guns? It isn't a hunt. It's a game, like Coffin said, and one must win the game and one must lose. And the ultimate price paid in losing was the life of the animal.

When Andy considered what Coffin had said he thought of the man as a complete enigma. He had been surprised and dismayed at the apparent cruelty displayed by the hunter. He had killed that wolf with complete disdain. He showed none of the sympathy towards the desperate animal that he had professed at their meeting in Fairbanks.

He thought suddenly of Max. He was still worried about him. The disturbed, pained expression that seemed to haunt Max had reappeared. Andy could not tell if it was the sickness he suspected that was now bothering Max or distress from Giff's revelation about what Max had done.

Andy was bruised by the revelation that it was Max alone who had purchased the paintings he had sold so far. Had Giff not revealed what Max had done it was logical to assume that Max would have arranged for all the paintings in future shows to be purchased. He felt disheartened. In his estimation he really had failed. None of his works had sold on its own merit. Max had made a bad decision. He had acted with misguided judgment. It probably was the only way he knew to express his love. All his life Max had used money and power as a projection of his affection. Good or bad, he believed Max had acted out of love for him. At least now that he knew what Max was up to any new shows would have to stand on the merits of his paintings.

Andy felt a sudden wave of remorse. Suppose Max really was seriously ill. It would be just like him to keep silent. He felt sorry that he had not been closer to Max over the years; sorry that he couldn't have given him what he wanted while there was time.

The sun finally came up but it was blocked by a low overlay of leaden gray cloud. It had grown damp and colder. The combination of cold air and moisture was certain to bring snow. As the snowmobiles churned along, Andy sensed sudden exhilaration. His concerned mood changed. The cold air filled his lungs, making him feel euphoric, with an attitude toward the wilderness he had not yet experienced. For a passing instant he felt akin to nature, a part of it. His head spun with the thought. Was this what the true hunter felt, he wondered. Could there actually be a spiritual bond that linked man and his environment? Was that what Giff knew and felt all along? He shrugged off the thought. Coffin, yes. But not Giff. He didn't believe Giff was capable of understanding such an emotion.

Was this the truth of nature, animals living in harmony with their environment? They functioned with a unity that adhered to the ageless pattern of give and take. Left alone, they would replenish and survive for all time. Was man, on the other hand, on a path of self destruction? Man used his environment with abandon, his immediate need his only goal. He polluted the atmosphere, raped the seas and stripped the earth with an ever-increasing demand for more. Man did not acknowledge, as animals did, a relationship with his habitat. Man spent his life trying to conquer nature, to tame it, to control it for his own use. The animal accepted being part of it.

The thought occurred to him, though, that animals were absolutely cruel in order to survive. Were they any different from the men who hunted them? The big fish ate the little fish. The stronger animal killed the weaker for food, as did man. But animals killed without conscience. Their only reason for slaughter was to fill their stomachs. He thought of the wolves who ate the bodies of their own in order to survive. Where did man differ in attitude? Man did pollute. Why? In order to survive in his own manner. Even the beaver tore down trees to build his shelter.

"It's sort of like being in church," Andy said. "Makes you contemplate your own existence."

Coffin smiled warmly and glanced back at Andy. "It is that," he remarked.

Andy suddenly felt ashamed. He had not meant to express his thoughts.

"I was thinking out loud," he said. "Sorry."

"Nothing to apologize for," Coffin said. "You're right. This is the true house of God."

Andy's simple statement had exposed a profundity in Coffin Andy suspected might be there. He hadn't seen it manifest itself until now.

"It's going to snow," Coffin said. "Maybe in a few hours. We're going to have to quit before it starts. We can't risk being caught out in a storm."

"Will it be bad?" Andy asked.

"Hard to say. Could be. Radio said about six inches. But you never know. Those clouds on the horizon look heavy."

"You'd call off the hunt?"

"For today. Yes. We can't hunt in a storm. The wolf pack would take shelter anyhow. We wouldn't be able to track them. We'd head back to the lodge till it blows over."

"Giff isn't going to like that," Andy said.

"He'll have to like it," Coffin said.

It took the snowmobiles less than an hour to cover the fifteen miles it had taken the wolf pack hours to traverse. The gray clouds still hung low and threatening but it hadn't started to snow yet. The wolf pack's trail was still clearly defined and easy to follow. The winding rut in the blue-white snow pointed the way unerringly.

* * *

The wolves slept for four hours, a sleep they badly needed. They would soon return to the area of their den, some eighteen miles to the south.

Midnight awoke to the now familiar droning sounds of the snowmobiles which immediately struck terror in his heart. The men were closing on them again. The wolves awoke and cocked their heads, their ears straining to pick up the direction of the sound. Midnight sniffed the air to catch the scent of the men, but detected no smell. Their adversaries were downwind from the pack and unknowingly had a slight advantage over the wolves.

The wolves had slept in a cluster of thick spruce at the rim of a woodland. If they had merely moved deeper into the thicket they would not be seen from the direction the men traveled. But the woods backed into a high, almost vertical ridge of snow-covered rock that cut off escape to the rear. The tracks they left in the snow led directly to their present position. If they remained where they were they would surely be trapped and picked off one-by-one by the hunters. Their only hope for escape was to put immediate distance between themselves and the men.

The pack would have to move farther into unfamiliar territory in order to escape certain death. Midnight had spent his first months in the wilderness traversing the open terrain. He had covered thousands of square miles and had learned how to expertly cope with changing conditions and new landscapes and perils. But the pack had never strayed beyond their own self-imposed boundaries. They would be confused and terrified without Midnight to guide them.

Midnight stood up and shook the snow from his thick, glistening black coat. Quickly assuming the role of alpha animal, he brought the pack out of the shallow woods in the open. They headed west, skirting an outcropping ridge of rock that cut off the pack's route. Midnight stayed close to the perimeter of trees and followed them to the end of the ridge. The wolves came to a glade that dropped off with a sharp incline to a river fifty feet below. If the wolves could make it across the glade and down the incline they might make it to safety. The narrow river below, partially frozen over, wound its snakelike way into a dense forest. It was their only safety for they were now cut off by the men behind them.

If they made it inside the dense forest the wolves would easily outdistance the men. They could move through the woods and emerge miles from their pursuers.

Midnight made his choice and, ultimately, made a mistake. He crossed the open field, the pack close behind him, in a mad rush for the embankment.

The noise of the snowmobile engines was louder then ever, the steady hum becoming a roar, as the pack was surprised by the gleaming metallic monsters charging right at them over the crest of a long, low hill.

*   *   *

The surprise of seeing the wolf pack so close to them jolted Andy out of his reverie and instantly woke him to reality. As the machines churned through the snow he had become absorbed in thoughts about his art, Max, Coffin, Giff and the animals who were going to die today. It was a confused, disassembled array of images and events that had no focus, only confusion and a notion that he had to find answers to the questions that bothered him. How important was his relationship to Max? And Giff? Did it really matter that Max had bought all his work? And what the hell was he doing here?

The machines bounced smoothly along for miles, staying in the trail set down by Midnight and the wolf pack. It finally started to snow, the soft flakes falling slowly to the already white surface of the ground. The machines crossed over the swell of a hill that blocked all but the sky from view. As the men shot over the top they saw the wolves a few hundred yards from them.

"My God!" Giff cried. "There they are!"

Before any commands were given by the men operating the snowmobiles Giff raised his weapon and fired. The shots were premature and fell short of their intended target. The slugs harmlessly disappeared in the snow.

"Hold it!" Coffin cried out. "Wait 'til we get closer."

But Giff was no longer heeding Coffin's orders. He had decided he would make his own decisions concerning the death of the wolves. He was not going to miss out on the prize he wanted. He was afraid Coffin would gun down the wolf before he could get to it. He had his shotgun aimed and poised again, ready to fire.

The third machine carrying Max and Mason pulled alongside Giff's and the three snowmobiles were now abreast of one another. Coffin waved to Giff to lower the gun. Giff frowned. The others were watching him. Slowly, reluctantly, Giff lowered the gun, its barrel pointed away from the center of activity, but his face showed his annoyance. Giff had sense enough not to risk firing with the men gathered so close to him.

The wolves turned and ran away from the oncoming machines, but they were quickly overrun. In an instant the three machines had closed around the trailing wolves. Giff was yelling at Fuller to continue on after the lead wolf.

"The black one!" he cried. "Catch up to the black one!"

Fuller responded to Giff's command and pulled ahead of the others, passing the trailing wolves as he chased Midnight in the lead.

"Damn it!" Andy heard Coffin swear. "He's going for the leader."

Midnight was suddenly caught in a desperate situation. He had allowed himself and the pack to be trapped in the open. The odds against directing the pack to safety were definitely against the wolves.

The fact that the wolves had eaten and slept temporarily replenished their energy. Right now they were in slightly better physical condition than they were the previous day. Their leader was courageous and willing to attack any adversary.

Midnight saw the machines getting closer. The pack was flanked on both sides and being driven to the edge of the ravine. Midnight faltered, stumbling in the snow, costing him valuable steps. The machines were upon him. Giff had his shotgun raised and was taking aim for the kill.

Coffin sped up his machine and swiftly pulled ahead of the stumbling lead wolf. Midnight was low in the snow and struggled to regain his footing. The white wolf was directly behind him and gaining on her mate. She was about to overrun him. Coffin turned inward and cut between the black wolf and his white mate. He angled the snowmobile to his left and was quickly in position to block Giff from getting a clear shot at the black wolf. Coffin held his snowmobile steady as Giff's machine pulled astride.

"Get the hell out of the way!" Giff screamed at Coffin. "What do you think you're doing?"

"Not this one!" Coffin cried out. "He's not going to be your trophy."

By now Midnight had regained control. He was up on all fours and not about to die without a battle. He turned to face his enemy, the man nearest him. Moon was running behind him and she had slowed considerably. If the wolves didn't get out of this trap they would all be dead very soon. Midnight moved swiftly. He leaped at the men on the machine directly in front of him.

Coffin had his back to Midnight when the wolf leaped. He was facing Giff. Andy saw Midnight charging. He couldn't believe the wolf would have the courage to attack in the face of certain death. Andy saw the animal's giant incisor teeth exposed as his lips curled back in a vicious snarl. His green eyes gleamed as he charged. The black wolf moved so fast Andy did not respond in time.

Midnight hit Andy with terrific force and tore him from his seat. Andy fell on his back in the snow, the large wolf on top of him. He feared for his life and tried to fight off the wolf with his hands. The animal seemed much larger and more ferocious than he imagined. The wide, gaping mouth and the huge teeth were terrifyingly close. Andy crossed his arm over his face in an attempt to protect his throat. In an instant, the massive, powerful jaws clamped on his left arm and closed tight. The wolf dragged him from the machine in the snow, tearing at his arm.

It all happened in an instant. Giff reacted in the seconds that elapsed. He lifted his shotgun for a clear shot at Midnight but was blocked by Coffin's snowmobile. Max, behind Coffin, saw the entire pack slow down as their leader charged the men on the machine. Max watched Andy fall in the snow. The old man panicked. He brought the shotgun to his shoulder and sent a volley at the wolves, firing wildly. He missed. The wolves paused at the sound of the explosion and ran away from the hunters. Max pumped the gun and fired again. And missed the wolves again.

Coffin had been knocked from the snowmobile when Midnight attacked. He rolled over on his stomach and yanked his .45 automatic from his holster. He snapped a round into the chamber and aimed at Midnight from a prone position. He couldn't get off a clear shot. Andy was between him and the wolf.

Midnight was mauling Andy. Coffin couldn't wait. He leaped to his feet to get above his target for a clear shot. He fired without aiming; once, twice, clipping the shots off his hip. One of the shots apparently hit the wolf for he rolled backward off Andy.

Giff, in the meantime, had left the snowmobile and trudged desperately through the snow to Andy and Coffin. He was still not in position for a good shot.

Moon was near enough to Midnight to respond to her mate's plight. She charged directly at Coffin as his gun barked its terrible noise. Coffin was about to fire again when the white wolf hit him. She tumbled on her back and scrambled for position for a second attack. Giff now had a clear shot. He braced, pumped the shotgun and fired. The wolf dropped in her tracks six feet from Coffin. Moon was dead.

Coffin turned to Giff. "Thanks," he called out.

Midnight had rolled off Andy and was running from the men.

Coffin dropped beside Andy. The boy was badly wounded. The wolf had swiftly and savagely torn open his left shoulder, bit-ing through layers of clothing. He was bleeding badly. Coffin dropped his pistol in the snow and cradled Andy in his arms. He had lost consciousness. Coffin pressed his right hand into the wound applying as much pressure as he could to halt the bleeding.

Midnight was increasing the distance between him and the men. The other wolves had already bolted over the slope and were well ahead of him as they scrambled down the embankment. Giff raised the shotgun and fired at the escaping black wolf. Midnight disappeared out of sight over the edge and was gone.

"I got him!" Giff shouted. "I swear I got the black wolf!"

He turned back to Andy and Coffin. He stumbled over to them.

"Damn!" he cried. "Kid looks terrible."

"Help me," Coffin said.

Max and the others had finally joined the men. When Max saw what had happened to Andy he dropped in the snow beside him.

"Oh God," he howled. "How bad is it?"

"Don't know yet. Doesn't look too good," Coffin said. "Wolf tore up his shoulder."

"He's not . . . dead?" Mason asked.

"No," Coffin answered. "He passed out."

Fuller got a first aid kit from one of the snowmobiles and brought it to Coffin. Together they cleaned and bandaged the wound as best they could. Andy was still bleeding but not as bad now.

"This isn't good," Fuller said. "We've got to get him to a hospital and have that wound taken care of properly."

"Can we radio for help?" Coffin asked.

"Sure. From the cabin."

"I'm going with you," Max said. "I want to stay with Andy."

"All right," Fuller said. "Let's get back to the cabin. It's starting to snow. We don't want to get caught if it gets worse."

Giff had trudged through the snow to the edge of the ravine, about three hundred feet away, while the others were occupied with Andy. He was at the edge of the embankment. He looked for Midnight where he would have tumbled to the bottom. There were many tracks in the snow leading into the shallow river and emerging on the other side. They led directly into the woods on that side of the river. Midnight was nowhere in sight. Giff had not hit him as he had thought and the black wolf had gotten away again.

"Giff!" Max cried out. "Come on. We've got to get Andy out of here."

"I'm trying to spot that black wolf," Giff yelled back.

"The hell with him. Get back here!" Max's voice blasted in the cold air.

Coffin and Fuller lashed Andy to the seat of the snowmobile and climbed aboard. Giff made his way back to the men.

"How is he?" Giff asked.

"He's weak," Fuller said. "Unconscious. We have to get him out of here."

"You go ahead," Giff said. "I'm taking this white wolf back with me. I'm not letting this beauty go. Mason knows the way back to the cabin. We'll catch up with you there."

"Giff, are you crazy?" Max cried. "The hell with the damn wolves. Andy's hurt."

"Go ahead, Max," Giff snapped. "Don't argue with me." He turned to Mason. "You and me," he ordered. "We're taking this wolf back with us. Let's get it lashed to the snowmobile."

Mason asked Fuller "What's going on?"

"Help him with the wolf. We haven't got time to argue," Fuller said, disgusted. "We'll meet at the cabin."

"Come on," Max said to Fuller. "We're losing time."

The men gunned the machines and sped off, leaving Giff and Mason with Moon's lifeless body.

"I don't like this," Mason said. "We should be leaving with the rest of the party."

"Get this wolf with me," Giff ordered. "We'll catch up to them without any trouble."

"There's a storm right on us. We could get caught out in it."
Giff was trying to lift Moon's body out of the snow.

"Christ, this weighs a ton," he said.

Mason reluctantly joined Giff. "Dead weight," he said. "And
the fur is soaked."

They got Moon draped over the front hood of the snowmobile
and lashed her tight. When they were finished Giff climbed on.
With the weight of the wolf, him and Mason the machine dug
deeper into the snow and slowed them down.

"Hell," Giff said, "it isn't that bad. We're only about an hour
behind them."

Mason had no trouble following the tracks made by the snowmobiles ahead of them. The machines were not in sight because
the increasing snowfall cut down visibility and they had to rely
solely on the tracks. By the time they got to the spike cabins the
storm hit.

CHAPTER 22

When Fuller and Coffin arrived at the cabins they immediately brought Andy inside and laid him on one of the bunks. He was still unconscious, but the bleeding had stopped. The fresh snow was now a few inches deeper than when they had left in the morning and was still falling heavily.

Fuller got on his radio and called for help. His first attempt was to get an emergency helicopter to fly in and transport Andy to the nearest hospital. But the helicopter service would not come during the storm. They would have to wait until it broke. He was informed it would be at least twenty-four hours. His second attempt was also a failure. He tried to contact local rangers who had better equipment than theirs to make it through the storm. They at least offered advice in treating Andy until conditions got better.

"This is terrible," Max said. "What else can we do?"

"All we have are the snowmobiles and the radio," Fuller said. "We can lash Andy to the seat of one, cover him and try to make it to the lodge and wait there until the storm breaks. Personally, I think we'd be better off waiting right here."

"Why?" Max asked. "Aren't we losing time?"

"We lose time either way," Fuller answered. "We can't fly out and no one can fly in. If we go out in the storm it might be worse for the boy. And God help him if we break down along the way."

"All right," Max said. "I'll take your word. Let's hope for the best."

"We have plenty of water, food and first-aid material. We'll stay on the radio all the time."

The cabin door burst open, spilling Giff and Mason into the room.

"Storm's getting bad," Mason exclaimed. "What are the plans?"

"We have to wait out the storm here," Fuller said. "Then we either head for the lodge or wait here for a helicopter. Coffin can fly Andy out once we know whether or not we can get a helicopter in."

"Sounds like a chopper is the best bet," Giff interjected. "Would they come straight here?"

"I think so, if they had to," Fuller answered. "There's enough clearing for them to land."

"Then let's push for the helicopter," Max said. "If it's a problem of money, don't worry. Our only concern right now is Andy."

Giff shook the snow from his jacket and moved closer to the fireplace. He pulled a pack of cigarettes from a pocket and lit one. "We ought to let him pay for any bills," Giff said, pointing to Coffin. "He caused Andy to get hurt."

Coffin had said nothing since they returned. He was aware that he had implemented the action which resulted in Andy's injury. His obsession with saving Midnight for his own brand of justice, his overwhelming need to see the black wolf die by his own hand, in his own time frame, had altered his judgment in a critical situation. He knew what might happen when a wolf was fighting for his life. He knew any wolf would kill to survive. He was the so-called expert. He should not have let his own personal agenda influence his ability to make correct decisions in a crisis. He was responsible for the safety of the men he guided. He had accepted the responsibility and had failed.

Giff was right. Andy was injured because of his interference. He faced Max Taylor and looked directly into his eyes. He wasn't sure what he wanted to see there.

"Your son is right," he said. "This was my fault. I could have gotten the boy killed."

"Why?" Max said. "Why did you cut Giff off from the black wolf?"

"I didn't want Giff to kill the wolf," Coffin said. "I wanted the wolf to live."

"What the hell for?" Giff snapped. "We're here on a hunt. You were hired by us. We have a right to shoot any wolf. What's so special about this wolf?"

"I was saving him for myself," Coffin said.

"Why you miserable son of a bitch!" Giff cursed. "I knew you were up to something. Who the hell do you think you are?"

"Look," Coffin said. "I don't blame you. The wolf's name is Midnight. He was my wolf."

"Your wolf," Max exclaimed. "What are you talking about?"

"I raised him from a pup. I used to keep a wolf pack on my property. Midnight became the alpha wolf."

"You raised wolves?" Giff questioned.

"For a while. My wife and I studied them."

"How did the wolf get here?" Max asked. "Did he escape?"

"Something went wrong," Coffin answered. "I was away and my wife was home with the wolves. They were always fenced, penned up, with room to roam. During a storm the wolves panicked. When my wife tried to help them they attacked her. The black one, Midnight, killed her."

"Good God," Max said. "No wonder you wanted him for yourself."

"I know there isn't much I can do to change what has happened," Coffin said. "But I want you to know I'm sorry. I would not have done anything to deliberately hurt the boy."

Giff crushed his cigarette out under his foot, turned away from Coffin and opened the front door.

"Someone help me get this white wolf off the snowmobile," he said.

Fuller went out with him. Together they lifted Moon off the machine and got her to the wall of the cabin. The carcass was heavy and awkward. Mason came out to help them. He lashed the wolf's hind legs together. They lifted the body and hooked the bound legs over a metal hook which protruded from the wall. The white carcass hung upside down. Drops of blood leaked from the wounds and fell to the snow.

"He's a mean-looking animal," Giff said. "Imagine what that black wolf must look like."

"She," Fuller said. "This one's a female. Probably the black wolf's mate."

"Goddamn," Giff said. "I shot a female."

*   *   *

Midnight was confused and frightened. He ran away from the terrible sounds that brought death to the pack, charging through the heavy snow with a relentless determination to live. He trudged on blindly, without direction or destination. He felt pain in his right rump but was able to move without great difficulty. Something has caused him to hurt and he associated the pain with the men. The madly fleeing pack, scattered by the men's onslaught, followed Midnight and soon reassembled closely behind him in the dense woods across the river.

Midnight pushed on, trampling down the snow, breaking a trail. After running for a long while his fear finally subsided. Death no longer pursued him. But Moon was not with him. She had stayed behind where death lingered. He felt that his mate was harmed. His sense for survival had taken him away from the slaughter but dread for his mate had given him reason to fear again.

The remaining members of the pack gathered around him beneath an overgrowth of fir trees and, in the shower of falling snow, they howled their fearful cries for hours.

*   *   *

The snow was still falling when Midnight led the wolves back to the place where the men had killed Moon. Her scent was weak in the new snow and it was mingled with another scent, that of man. The trail of his mate's blood was barely discernible in the snow and it ended after he followed it for a few yards. At that point a new trail had been carved out by the men's machines.

Midnight set off along the flattened trail, urged on by an instinct stronger than the fear of dying. He had to find Moon and bring the pack to her. He resumed his trek through the falling snow, the wolves willingly following him. The remainder of the pack, which now numbered eight, accepted his authority without hesitation.

As the evening neared and the sun vanished, the wolves pushed forward, carving a wearisome path along the way. The snow piled deeper, and, by the time they reached the spike cabins, the smell of Moon was stronger near the men's lair. It was carried on the wind and filled Midnight's nostrils. She was very near.

Midnight was tired and stumbled through the steadily deepening snow. The other wolves behind him were equally tired and were bumping into one another as they plodded onward. He brought the pack directly into the raw face of danger to find his mate. He discovered her dangling upside down on the wall of one of the cabins. He drew closer to her and sniffed her lifeless body. The sense that Moon was dead suddenly devastated the black wolf. He slumped and rolled in the spot where Moon's blood still slowly dripped to the blemished snow. He began to wail, a mournful cry that was soon taken up by the pack. Their howling hung on the frosted air and pronounced their dreadful loss.

*   *   *

Coffin had fallen into a state of numbed silence. He sat on the edge of a bunk while Max and Giff were at the table in the small cabin. The fire was kept burning as logs were added throughout the night. Fuller and Mason were in the second cabin. The men had settled down and became quiet, each absorbed in his own thoughts. It was not a time for idle conversation. They were aware of the seriousness of the situation.

The woeful howling of the wolves suddenly broke the silence. "Listen to that!" Giff exclaimed. "Wolves."

"I hear," Max said. "They're close. What's going on?"

Giff got up from the table and went to the lone window in the cabin. It was frosted over. He wiped a clear spot and peered out.

"I'll be damned!" he swore. "Will you look at this. It's the wolves. They're right outside the cabin. They must have followed us through the storm."

"What?" Max cried, jumping to his feet. "What do they want?"

Coffin joined them at the window. They strained to see outside. There, spotted in the white landscape, through the haze of the falling snow, was the remainder of the wolf pack. In front was the looming black silhouette of Midnight.

"Goddamn wolves!" Max swore. "They're as crazy as we are."

*   *   *

Midnight approached the lifeless body of his mate. The remaining members of the pack followed close behind him, aware of the impending danger from the hunters who were nearby. The black wolf clenched his jaws around Moon's dangling paws. He pulled downward with all his weight. The subordinate wolves followed Midnight's actions and joined his attempts to dislodge Moon's body from its perch on the cabin wall. The wolves were soon frustrated and whipped into a frenzy. The white wolf's body would not come loose. They began to hurl themselves at the carcass in an effort to release it from the wall. They rocked the dead hulk by repeatedly crashing into it. Still, it would not fall to the ground. It was as if Midnight and his pack expected Moon to get up and walk away with them if they could only get her off the wall.

Each time a wolf struck Moon the force of the hurtling body crashing against the wall knocked loose a rain of snow. Inside the cabin the men became disconcerted by the sounds of wolves slamming into the cabin.

"What the hell is going on?" Max swore. "What are they doing?"

Giff was still at the window with his face pressed close against it.

"Son of a bitch!" he cried. "You won't believe this. They're trying to get the white wolf off the wall."

The men watched in awe. They were fascinated by the heroic attempts of the wolf pack to redeem the alpha female's corpse.

Giff left Max and Coffin at the window and lifted his coat from the bunk. He slipped the .44 from its holster where it hung on the bunk post. He made sure it was loaded and stepped out the cabin door before the others realized what he was doing.

Outside, Midnight had retreated from his task and rested momentarily in the deep snow against the cabin wall. He squatted down, letting his body settle into the soft, cold surface. The pack still vainly tried to resurrect Moon while Midnight rested.

Suddenly the front door of the cabin burst open. In the yellow light from inside, Giff stood silhouetted, his legs spread apart, the silvery gun held outward in his hand. It pointed at the struggling wolves. Midnight was less than fifteen feet from Giff who didn't see him against the cabin wall. He was concentrated on the other wolves grouped around the white wolf.

It all happened in a few seconds. Giff pointed the .44 at the wolves and it exploded twice. Moon's female offspring was dead the instant the bullets struck her. She was thrown backward by the impact and hurled to the trampled snow. The weapon crashed again and another wolf died.

Giff was laughing aloud. The wolves had been gathered in a tight cluster around Moon's body. They were still trying to rip the carcass off the wall when he emerged from the cabin. He had fired twice at the first wolf. A mistake, he thought. He could have taken it out with only one shot. Max should be right behind him.

Inside the cabin the men reacted quickly when they heard the shots and saw Giff standing outside the open door. Coffin saw Max rushing to get a weapon so he grabbed a shotgun and ran out the door.

Midnight reacted swiftly after the last shot felled the second wolf. He leaped out of the snow and charged the man before the sound of death could bark again. He hit Giff full force. The .44 flew from Giff's hand and dropped in the snow. The thrust of Midnight's forward motion drove Giff down to the frozen surface. The wolf tried to get at the man's throat but Giff threw his arms above his face. The great jaws closed over his outstretched arm and ripped at him. Giff screamed.

The other wolves saw their leader attack an enemy and instantly joined the assault. They pounced on Giff as Midnight backed off. Coffin came out of the cabin and saw Giff struggling with the wolves. He quickly raised the shotgun to his shoulder. A gray animal had Giff by the jacket and was dragging him through the snow. Coffin couldn't fire. With the wolves so close to Giff he might hit him instead of the animal.

Max appeared beside Coffin. He raised his shotgun to fire but couldn't get a shot off.

"Damn!" he cursed.

Coffin moved swiftly. Not a second to spare. He gripped the shotgun by the barrel and charged into the wolves who surrounded Giff. He swung the weapon with brute force at the animals, driving howling wolves scurrying away in pain.

Behind them, as Max prepared to fire at the retreating wolves, Midnight struck Max from the rear and knocked him down. In an instant the jaws of the powerful wolf gripped the elder man behind the neck and crushed his windpipe. Midnight struck so quickly neither Coffin nor Giff had a chance to respond. They had their hands full with the wolves who were again charging them. Giff got to his feet. He quickly retrieved his fallen gun. He snapped off a shot at Midnight and missed as the black wolf scampered off into the storm.

Coffin lifted his shotgun to his shoulder, pumped and fired at a charging gray wolf. The hammer clicked on an empty chamber. He realized in an instant what had happened. The ammunition was in the pockets of his coat which was inside the cabin. He had run to Giff's assistance without it. Coffin swung the shotgun violently trying to back the wolves up. Giff fired his last shot and a wolf dropped in front of him.

The door of the second spike cabin flew open and Fuller and Mason emerged, shotguns poised. They fired at the wolves. Fuller hit one that fell dead. The remaining wolves ran off into the night.

"God damn!" Fuller exclaimed. "What the hell happened?"

"Wolves charged the cabin," Coffin said. He went to Max, Giff by his side. They knelt over Max.

"My God!" Giff cried. "Is he dead?"

Coffin felt for a pulse and heartbeat. There was none. He nodded to Giff. "Dead."

"God almighty!" Giff cried in distress. "What have I done? He followed me out the door. Tried to help me."

The men carried Max inside the spike cabin. Andy was sitting up on the bunk, clutching his damaged arm. He struggled to stay upright. "What . . . happened?" he managed to say.

Giff answered. "Max has been hurt. Damn black wolf got him."

"Bad. . . ?" Andy questioned and dropped back on the bunk.

Giff nodded. "The worst. He's dead."

They laid Max on a table and wrapped his wounds. He was lifeless.

"My damn fault," Giff admonished himself. "I shouldn't have gone outside and started shooting. I didn't think what could happen."

"Let me see that arm," Fuller said to Giff. They got his torn jacket off and Giff rolled up his sleeve. "You were lucky," Fuller said. "He didn't break the skin but your arm is going to be sore as hell."

"Lucky?" Giff said. "My father is dead. I did it. I caused it."

The men fell silent. Everything happened within the span of only a few minutes. Four wolves and one man were dead.

* * *

In the morning a helicopter arrived once the storm had passed. Max and Andy were flown to Fort Yukon. Max's body would be shipped to New York City. Andy was given immediate medical attention and he would leave for surgery. Giff made all the arrangements by phone. He stayed behind with Coffin and the hunters.

When they made it back to the lodge they found the storm had piled drifts of snow around Coffin's plane that made it impossible to take off. It would take hours to dig it out.

"I've got to get back to New York," Giff said to the three men. "But I figure I've got a couple of days left. I'd like to continue after that black wolf."

"Why don't we call it quits," Fuller said. "We've got to skin a lot of wolves. We've got dead wolves all around the cabins. I've no heart in continuing."

"Keep the wolves," Giff said. "I don't want any of them. I just want to finish this."

"It's finished for us," Fuller said. "I don't want any more. Your brother's hurt and your father's dead."

"I'm aware of that. But now, I owe that black wolf," Giff declared. "Just like Coffin. We've each got a good reason to kill that bastard wolf. There's plenty of time left to get him."

"This thing has gotten out of hand," Fuller said. "It doesn't make sense anymore. How do you think we feel about all that's happened?"

"I understand your dilemma," Giff said. "But understand how I feel. That wolf killed my father."

"I'm responsible," Fuller said. "I'll have to answer to the authorities for all that's happened."

"I'll take all the responsibility for what has happened," Giff declared. "And don't worry about the money end of it."

Fuller fell silent.

"How about you?" he asked, turning to Coffin. "You and me. We go after the black wolf together. We can handle it. Just the two of us."

"I don't think so," Coffin said. "You're not in the best shape right now."

"I'm fine. The arm feels fine," Giff said. "I owe you for getting those wolves off me. Thanks."

"You'd have done the same for me," Coffin said.

"Well, do we go after the black wolf?" Giff persisted.

"Look," Coffin said, "right now I think Fuller is right. Maybe another time I might consider it. But that wolf pack is destroyed. Lord knows where Midnight will be in the next few days."

"That's my point," Giff said. "Now is the time to get him."

"I'll fly you down to Fairbanks," Coffin said. "You can get a plane out from there."

"Is it money? I'm willing to pay. I mean some real money."

"It's not money," Coffin said. "Believe me."

"It's because of your wife," Giff persisted. "The black wolf, what he did to her. You want him yourself."

It took a minute for Coffin to respond. "You're right. I'll probably spend the rest of my life hunting him."

"Damn," Giff said. "Let me help you. We'll never get a better chance. He's close enough for us to track him. You kill him. I don't care. I just want to be part of it."

*   *   *

Midnight ran off into the blinding storm, hurt and bleeding. He had been clubbed by the man who had once held him in captivity. The man had broken the skin and chipped a bone in his shoulder. He had been grazed with a bullet in the rump; the wound was sore and forced him to favor his left hind quarter. But he pushed on into the snowy night to escape with his life. The battle was lost. The wolf pack was all but wiped out. Behind him, the three wolves followed in a single file. The pack had been decimated by the men and their terrible instruments of death. There was no hope for Moon and any of the wolves who tried so valiantly to save her. So many would never return to their territory again. The few remaining wolves could no longer function as a pack. They would have to recruit other wolves to join them. Midnight would have to find a new alpha female to mate with him to rebuild the quality of a new pack.

He pushed on, covering as much distance as he could before the night fell, driving the three wolves until they could no longer continue. He took them deep into the woods and together they rested while the storm blew itself out.

CHAPTER 23

Fuller, Mason and Giff helped Coffin dig his plane out of the snow. Together they moved it to the clearing where he would take off. The Piper Cub lifted off and pulled away. Coffin guided the plane expertly over the surrounding tree tops and banked in a slow circle. Giff sat beside him in the passenger seat. They had piled their gear and guns behind the seats.

"I never expected it to end like this," Giff said, resigned to the fact that the hunt was over. "I screwed up big time. I dragged Max out of the cabin and that black wolf killed him."

Coffin was silent for a few moments. He turned to Giff, considering him. "I'm heading north," he announced. "I'll give it one last try. Maybe we'll get lucky."

"You're going after the black wolf?" Giff exclaimed, obviously excited. "Damn. Let's do it."

"There aren't many wolves left," Coffin said. "Three or four. They still have to hunt. We might catch them in the open. It's the only chance we've got. If they stay in the woods we'll miss them. I think I hit Midnight. He could be wounded and running slower."

"How are we going to work this?" Giff asked. "How do we fly and shoot at the same time?"

"I fly, you shoot," Coffin said. "You open the window on your side and use a shotgun."

Giff was astounded. "You don't care if I kill the wolf?"

"It doesn't matter anymore," Coffin said. "Dead is dead."

Giff was elated. He remained calm, not wanting to expose his emotion to Coffin. His kill, he thought. His trophy! He reached behind him and brought a shotgun to the front. He loaded it and pumped a round into the chamber.

Coffin is a strange guy, Giff thought. The wolf hunter still resented him yet he buried his animosity because of the circumstances. He was fully in Coffin's hands now. Giff had thought of himself as a leader but, in his heart, he knew he had lived in his father's shadow. He was no different from any of the wolves in a pack, following the leader. That leader was Max; always had been. And now he was being led by Coffin.

Still, he considered himself lucky to be Max's son. That distinction brought the power he had enjoyed all his life and that position made his life everything he wanted it to be. Thank God it would never change and would only get better.

Coffin aimed the plane north towards the spike cabins. From there he would be able to get to the territory Midnight and his wolves marked as theirs. It wouldn't take much time to fly over open areas looking for the remaining wolves. He stayed low, buzzing over the tree tops, careful to keep high enough not to clip them, yet staying low enough to spot the wolves.

Soon he flew over the area where Midnight had mauled Andy. The storm had obliterated all traces of the confrontation. The plane crossed the river where the wolves had gone into the woods. Coffin skimmed over the trees and came to a glade where the trees ended. He brought the small plane still lower and skirted the edge of the woodland.

In the fresh snow there was a clear trail coming from the woods. Coffin swooped down and followed the tracks the wolves had made. Flying low, it was easy to follow in the wide clearing.

And then, abruptly, ahead, the men saw them. Midnight was

leading three wolves in a straight line across the snow. After the storm, the snowfall was soft and deep. The wolves stumbled and fought to keep moving.

"Get ready," Coffin said. "Open the window."

Giff complied and lifted the shotgun into position. "Are we going to hit him from this high up?" he asked Coffin.

"Don't worry," Coffin replied. "We're going down. Hold on to your socks."

Coffin dipped the plane and zoomed over the wolves, no more than twenty feet above them. He kept the wolves to the right of the plane in plain sight so that Giff could get a clear shot. The ground came up like an eruption, faster and more frightening than Giff imagined. They passed over the wolves before he could get a clear shot.

"Damn it," Giff cried. "I blew it. I'm not used to this."

"We'll do it again," Coffin said.

The wolves below were terrified. They sensed death coming from man, this time from the sky. It was the noise that men brought with them and its meaning was devastating.

Coffin brought the plane around again, cutting his circle tighter this time. Giff braced himself. The wolves grew larger as the plane closed in on them. It seemed to Giff that they were riding right on the snow as the wolves' shapes loomed just ahead of them. He aimed, fired, pumped the gun swiftly and fired again. One of the gray wolves running behind Midnight dropped. Midnight broke to the left and ran under the plane.

"Got one!" Giff cried out.

"We only want Midnight," Coffin said. "The hell with the other wolves. One more time around."

He banked again, made a slow, wider circle and came in at the wolves head on.

"I'm coming right at them this time," Coffin said.

"Okay. I'm ready."

Here came the wolves. The plane was so low the animals appeared to be running right at them. Coffin was no more than six feet off the ground. Giff fired at Midnight. He missed, pumped again but never got the chance to fire again.

Something hit the plane with a jolt and it pitched forward crazily. Coffin fought to keep the nose up but a sudden force was dragging on it. One of the wolves had attacked the plane as it passed over them. He had leaped at the enemy and his powerful jaws clamped onto the right ski, driving his incisors deep into the wood. The wolf could not unlock his jaws and his weight dragged down on the low-flying airplane.

The plane wobbled viciously as Coffin struggled with the controls. He could not gain height. The snow-swept surface raced by. They were held parallel to the ground by the weight of the wolf.

"What's happening!?" cried Giff. "What's happening?"

"We hit something under us!" Coffin exclaimed.

Ahead, the snow ended on the bank of a winding river which carved a path through the valley. The other side of the river was bordered by the forest and a wall of cliff. Coffin had to react immediately. He had lost speed. He strained with all his might to get the plane up.

"Come on!" he swore. "Get up! Get up!"

Too late. He could not avoid a crash. The river flowed to a waterfall that dropped thirty feet to white water below. The plane was coming into the right bank and the head of the falls was directly ahead. The plane hit the river where it joined the edge of the waterfall in an explosion of snow and water. The nose buried itself into the water and the plane stopped just short of going over the falls. It hung tentatively on the edge, the tail sticking almost straight up in the air, lodged on the precipice.

The force of the collision killed the courageous wolf, breaking his neck. He hung from the shattered ski, his fangs still embedded in the splintered wood. The plane was sliding slowly over the edge of the falls, inexorably pushed by the rushing water. The left wing had cracked apart and the props were bent out of shape.

Giff was knocked unconscious on impact, his body going limp. Coffin was groggy, his head bloodied as it hit the cabin window.

Both men were already up to the their knees in water. Coffin cupped his head in his hands, trying to clear his brain. It took him a few long minutes to come around.

Coffin realized the danger to both him and Giff. They had only moments, maybe seconds, to get out of the plane before it went over the falls. The cascading water was forcing the plane higher as the nose wedged into the rocks at the edge.

Coffin couldn't tell how badly Giff was hurt. He didn't have time to examine him. He unbuckled Giff's seat belt and kicked open the door on his side. The plane was only twenty feet from the shoreline. If he could drag Giff out and get him clear before the plane went over, they had a chance of surviving the crash.

He reached over and pulled Giff toward him. Giff moaned, then cried out in pain.

"My leg," he cried. "I think it's broken."

"Lean into me," Coffin said. "We're in a bad spot. We crashed at the head of a waterfall. We're going over."

Giff glanced around quickly, surmising the dilemma.

"Damn!" he exclaimed as he eased out of the seat towards Coffin. Both men were kneeling on the instrument panel. "What happened?"

"I don't know," Coffin answered. He reached behind the seat and grabbed one of his packs and put his arm through the strap. "Hurry, there isn't much time."

The plane tipped forward with a lurch.

"We're going over!" Giff yelled.

Coffin got his arm around Giff's back and under his right shoulder and pulled with all the force he could gather. Giff pushed off with his right leg. The two men fell out of the door on the pilot's side, Coffin holding tight and making sure he dragged Giff with him. They hit the bitterly cold, rushing water along the edge of the falls clear of the plane as it went over.

Both men were in water almost to their knees and were pushed by the rushing force against the ledge at the head of the falls. Coffin got hold of Giff's jacket and pulled him towards him. He got a grip around Giff's arm and struggled along the rocky surface. Although they were close to the shore the force of the water was carrying them inevitably over the falls.

Coffin groped for solid footing and locked his arm around Giff. He slowly fought his way towards the river bank. But he was having difficulty holding on to Giff who could not find secure footing. The driving water pulled Giff over the edge. Coffin held on to the rocks with his left hand. He closed his grip tighter as he fell down. His body spread out flat on the rocky ledge of the falls, his right hand holding Giff as the water pounded over both men. He was losing his grip.

"Coffin," Giff cried out. "Coffin!"

Giff slipped away. He seemed to slide gracefully down the thirty-odd feet of cascading water into the bubbly torrent below. He went out of sight for a moment and came up struggling beneath the falls. Coffin got tentatively to his feet and surveyed the situation. The plane had landed upside down to the right of where Giff had fallen into the water. If he jumped from where he was there was plenty of room for him to make it without hitting the plane or Giff. Giff would not survive with a broken leg in the cold water. Coffin had to help him quickly. He made his decision. He stripped the pack from his shoulder and flung it with all his might to the shore below. It landed on the bank of the river well out of the way of the rushing water.

He leaped, feet first, out over the falls, and landed in the foam a few feet from Giff. The sudden shock of the cold water jolted Coffin like a mule kick to the chest. The water was over his head and he had to swim to Giff. He got an arm around him and both men fought for the shoreline, Coffin dragging Giff by his coat collar. The water was severely cold and they had to get out of it quickly. A man could live for only a few minutes in such cold water. Giff struck out in an attempt to swim, Coffin pushing and pulling him along. Finally, the two exhausted and freezing men collapsed on the snow-covered surface of the shore, gasping for air.

"We've got to get warm," Coffin gasped. "We'll freeze without a fire."

Giff reached into his jacket pocket and pulled out a Zippo lighter. He struck it open and clicked on a flame. "Damn, it works," he gasped.

Coffin foraged along the shoreline for wood. It took him only minutes to gather enough to get a fire started. He built it up and the two men huddled close to its warmth. Coffin got the backpack and opened it. It was his pack and he knew its contents. Inside were exactly what he needed; a canteen, a compass, an ax, a hunting knife, a few balls of heavy twine, gloves, extra pairs of socks, matches, a sweater, his .45 automatic and a package of cigars.

"The ax, the knife and the compass are what I wanted," Coffin said. "We'll need them to survive."

"I'd settle for a taxi cab right now," Giff said, grimacing in pain, trying to lighten their tense circumstance. "And room service."

"How's the leg feel?" Coffin asked.

"Not good," Giff grimaced.

"I've got to set it," Coffin said. He felt along Giff's leg with both hands. "It's not compound," he said. "But it appears to be fractured. It's swelling."

Coffin went along the shoreline of the river and after a while came back with a couple of long, straight branches. He hacked at them with the ax and formed two makeshift splints. He strapped them tightly to Giff's leg with the twine.

"Son of a bitch!" Giff cried in agony. "You're a heartless bastard!"

Coffin smiled. "Hang in there."

When they were both dry, Coffin filled the pack with only necessities. He filled the canteen with water from the river and cleaned and dried the .45, making sure it was in working condition.

"Don't throw out those cigars," Giff said. "I'd like one later."

"We've got to get going," Coffin said. "We've got a lot of ground to cover and we've got to get that leg of yours fixed properly."

"I can't walk," Giff said. "How are we going to get out of here?"

"Right now," Coffin said, "I'm going to carry you."

*   *   *

With Giff hung over his shoulders, Coffin moved along the bank of the river, past the waterfall. In the water was the Piper Cub. The plane had turned over and landed upside down. The dead wolf was still locked to the ski. His twisted body hung from the ski and seemed to be alive as the swiftly churning water moved him with its erratic rhythm. Coffin pointed to the plane.

"There's what brought the plane down," he told Giff.

"My God!" Giff exclaimed. "That wolf cracked us up? How could that happen?"

"He must have jumped at the plane and got hung up on the ski," Giff said. "It looks like his fangs are buried in the ski. Amazing animals, aren't they?"

Giff nodded in agreement. "Amazing."

*   *   *

Coffin was getting tired. They had to travel over twenty miles through both forest and glades. The snow was soft and deep in spots. There were patches of ice that made transit almost impossible at times. Without snowshoes Coffin sank deep into the snow with each step because of the weight he was carrying.

"Coffin," Giff said in his ear. "What happened to the black wolf?"

"Behind us," Coffin said calmly. "Along the tree line to the west."

"Goddamn!" Giff swore. He turned and looked back to where Coffin had indicated. He couldn't see Midnight anywhere. "I don't see him," Giff grunted.

"Oh, he's there. He's been following us for miles," Coffin assured him.

"What does he want?" Giff asked, suspecting the worst.

"He wants to kill us."

They had covered a few miles when Coffin could no longer continue. He carefully set Giff down when he struggled to a stand of birch trees on a slight rise. The snow was thinner here and, in some spots, the ground showed through.

"I've got to rest," Coffin said. "I'm not as young as I think I am."

"You're doing fine," Giff said, groaning as he held his leg.

Coffin collected some wood from the surrounding area, mostly dead branches which were drier and easier to burn. He got a fire going quickly and the men rested.

"We need food," Coffin said.

"What the hell are we going to do?" Giff asked. "We don't have a rifle. And I haven't seen any game."

"I'll go into the woods and see what I can get," Coffin said. "Maybe I'll get lucky."

He reached over and dropped the .45 automatic in Giff's lap. "You may need this," he said.

"What'll you hunt with?" Giff asked.

"I'll be all right. I've got the ax and a knife."

Giff tucked the pistol into his jacket pocket and watched Coffin go into the woods. He looked for the black wolf, but, again, he was nowhere to be seen. He wondered if the wolf was in the shelter of the trees waiting for Coffin. Giff thought that if he was going to get an effective shot at the wolf, he would have to let the animal get close to him. The pistol did not have the range of a rifle. What he wouldn't give for a .30-06 right now.

* * *

Coffin came out of the woods about an hour later carrying a snowshoe rabbit. Giff smiled when he saw what Coffin had.

"How the hell did you manage that so quickly?" he asked.

"Over the years you get to know the animals' tricks," Coffin replied.

They cooked the rabbit and ate. Coffin kept the fire going all the while.

"There's your wolf," Coffin suddenly said. "About four hundred yards along the edge of the woods."

This time Giff saw Midnight. He could just make out the distinctive shape of the large black wolf at the edge of the forest as he darted into the trees. He might not have seen him at all if the wolf had not moved. The light was fading as dusk was setting in.

"Why doesn't he give it up?" Giff stated.

"He doesn't like us," Coffin quipped.

Giff returned the .45 to Coffin. "We've got to keep moving," Coffin said calmly.

"Let me try to walk," Giff said. "Maybe we can find a branch I can use as a crutch."

"I'll carry you as long as I can," Coffin said. "I'll let you know when I can't."

"Then what do we do?"

"We'll figure something out when it becomes necessary," Coffin stated.

* * *

The weather remained clear. Coffin stopped to rest at intervals along the way rather than camp for the night. There was enough moonlight to guide him. In the woods he had to rely on the compass. But there was less snow on the ground and he made better time than in the open.

Coffin's shoulders and back were strained and sore, but it was his left foot that worried him most. He was afraid of frostbite. The cold was getting to him. He felt pain that would not go away.

He hadn't seen Midnight for a while. He wondered if he had given up yet, but he doubted it. The wolf was probably closer than he imagined. He would have to be on guard at all times, especially when they rested.

Neither man had spoken much over the last few miles, each absorbed in his own thoughts. The next time they rested Coffin said to Giff "I don't think I can carry you much farther."

"We're not going to make it, are we?" Giff said.

"The hell you say," Coffin admonished. "We'll get back."

Coffin gathered wood and built a fire. He cut two long straight saplings and shaped them into equal length poles. With the rolls of twine he shaped a web between the two poles and laced it with pine branches for strength.

Giff watched him, fascinated at the man's ingenuity and determination.

"Lie down on this on your back. It'll be easier this way," Coffin said. "I'll drag you the rest of the way, Indian style. It'll take the weight off my back." He helped Giff onto the structure and looped the twine he had attached to the poles over his shoulders.

"Pretty clever," Giff said.

"I don't know where the wolf is," Coffin said. "I lost him somewhere back there. He might be close to us in the woods. We'll have to be careful. He may have other wolves with him. I figure we've gone about nine or ten miles. From here on you rest while I'm walking. When we stop I'll try to sleep while you stay awake and watch. It's the only way we'll stay alive."

"Sounds good," Giff said. "Whatever you say, Coffin."

Coffin handed the .45 to Giff once again. "You stand watch. I'm going to get some sleep."

Coffin curled close to the fire while Giff sat on the ground next to him. The proximity to the fire kept them warm. There was enough wood to keep the fire alive for a few more hours. But they would need food again. They had traveled almost thirty-six hours and had covered, Coffin said, about nine miles. That would put their average rate at about a quarter mile an hour. They still had almost eleven miles to go. Could they last another three or four days, he wondered.

Coffin slept. He was snoring. Giff was amazed at the resolve and endurance of this man whom he had initially despised and now depended on for his life. His leg hurt tremendously but pride kept him from letting Coffin know just how bad he felt. And, in addition to his broken leg, he was developing a chest cold. From the dip in the water, he thought. A chill went through his body.

But not from the cold. He knew it was fear. For the first time in his life Giff felt the absolute fear of dying. He shrugged, purposefully trying to shake off the feeling.

Giff stared into the black haze of the night outside the rim of the fire. There's nothing out there to fear, he told himself. Was he imagining movement in the darkness? He lifted the .45 from his pocket, took off his glove and put his finger on the trigger. Just in case the black wolf had caught up to them.

And then, he saw something move. Was he seeing things or had something really moved out there in the snow? A vague shape, low to the ground, creeping through the night. The wolf? Then, to the left, another shape moved. He strained to see, to make sure. But the shapes were gone.

He snapped off the safety and tightened his grip on the .45. Should he wake Coffin or could he handle this himself? If he fired at the wolves the first shot would awaken Coffin. He wanted him to rest. It would be the wrong thing to do if he was hallucinating.

More shapes in the dark. And then nothing but the blackness of the night. Surely his eyes were playing tricks on him, deceiving him. His mind saw wolves where there were no wolves. Was it fear that made him see images?

No. There was movement. This time there could be no doubt. He saw a definite shape as it came toward him and then veered off into the night. He had seen it.

Where had it gone? Behind him?

Another wolf crossed in front of him. It was closer, moving slowly. A large gray wolf. Behind him was another, and another. They crossed each other's paths as they drew closer and closer.

Oh, God, he thought. What should he do?

He could make out definite features of the moving animals, their green eyes glowing, white fangs gleaming. They were no more than fifty feet away. But where was the black wolf? And there were too many wolves here. Where had they come from?

Giff raised the pistol and held it out with both hands, aimed

at the moving forms. Suddenly a dark shape burst out of the night
and charged right at him. He fired quickly. Surely he had hit the
wolf. But it was gone. He fired again at another shape and suddenly the .45 was wrenched from his hands.

Coffin was standing over him, clenching the pistol.

"What the hell are you shooting at?" he said.

"The wolves. Out there," Giff cried. "Behind you."

"Giff," Coffin grabbed him by the shoulders. "There's nothing there. Get hold of yourself. There are no wolves."

"What?"

"No wolves."

Giff realized he had panicked. He dropped his head in his
hands and began to sob. "Christ!" he sobbed. "I'm sorry, Coffin.
I'm seeing things."

"It's all right, kid," Coffin said. "It'll happen to anyone in
your condition."

"It was so damn real," Giff said. "I saw them all around us."

"Don't let it get to you," Coffin said, dropping his hand on
Giff's shoulder. "Let's get some rest."

*　*　*

Coffin was afraid Giff might be losing it, slipping into de-
lirium. He kept the .45 inside his own jacket rather than risk the
possibility that Giff might fire off any more wasted shots.

The two men rested by the fire. Giff drifted into sleep. It was
impossible to expect Giff to stand watch in his condition. Coffin
knew it was not going to be easy from here on. He would have to
catch short naps only under the safest conditions. Midnight was
out there and he would strike, given the opportunity.

Coffin propped himself up against the trunk of a birch tree
while Giff slept. He tried to convince his body that he was resting,
while he remained conscious. For a while it worked. The muscles
relaxed. He was not feeling the effort of either carrying Giff's dead
weight on his back or dragging it behind him. Coffin drifted into

sleep. The mind was attuned to the danger of slumber but could not fight the weariness that the body demanded be treated. Coffin fell asleep while Giff slept.

The subconscious took over. Thoughts buried there emerged slowly and were brought to the fore. Coffin saw the wolf in his mind. It was coming. He felt the danger and his mind forced him into consciousness.

His head snapped back as he was jolted awake.

His eyes opened. In front of him, inside the rim of the fire, outlined by its light, Midnight stood silently watching him. The wolf was no more than fifteen feet away, a distance he could cover in an instant.

Coffin kept absolutely still. He did not want to spook the wolf. Nor did he want Giff to suddenly awaken and see Midnight this close. A movement by either man might set the animal into a charge. What the hell was Midnight doing, Coffin thought. If he was able to get this close without much effort, he certainly could have struck Coffin as he dozed. Was he measuring them?

In the shadows, behind Midnight a gray wolf moved into the firelight. Both animals were crouched in adversarial positions and ready to spring. Coffin had to do something. If he could get the .45 out quickly enough he might get a shot at Midnight, but he doubted he could before the wolf hit him.

Right now, it was a standoff.

Perhaps, Coffin thought, Midnight was wary of the sounds of the two shots Giff had fired earlier. The wolf knew guns meant death. Yet why had he ventured so close without committing to a fight to the death? Perhaps he wanted to be certain it was Coffin he was stalking.

Coffin decided the only chance he and Giff had was to be daring.

"Midnight!" he said in a deep, booming voice. "Go away! Now!"

The wolf flinched, but did not move. Giff awakened at the sound of Coffin's voice. Coffin held his hand on Giff's arm and squeezed as Giff realized the danger. "Quiet," Coffin said softly. "Don't move."

"Midnight!" he loudly commanded the wolf again. "Go home! Damn it! Obey me! Go home!"

The wolf's liquid green eyes burned into Coffin's. He was making a decision.

Coffin dared not reach for the gun while the wolf stared him down.

"MIDNIGHT!" Coffin's voice boomed like a cannon shot. "GET THE FUCK OUT OF MY FACE!"

Suddenly, the wolf made his move. He bolted away and was gone into the depth of the night in an instant, taking the gray subordinate wolf with him. Coffin yanked the .45 out of his coat, pulled the glove from his hand and fired into the night in the direction the wolves had sped. One of the animals yelped in pain. Coffin fired again. Then he stopped, thinking better of wasting what few shots he had left by firing into the blackness. Midnight might be back. Or he might be wounded.

"Was he real?" Giff asked.

"He was real," Coffin assured him.

"Damn," Giff said. "That was some crap you pulled on that wolf. You bluffed him good. And the son of a bitch flinched."

"I'm glad it worked," Coffin said. "I didn't know what else to do. And I wasn't bluffing."

"You are some piece of work," Giff said, his pained smile beaming.

*   *   *

By the end of the third day Coffin had killed two more rabbits. He cooked the animals, and had to feed Giff. He was getting weaker and had developed a cough which was getting progressively worse.

Coffin could not increase his speed. He had to conserve his energy and concentrate on the last miles of the trip. But he wondered if Giff could make it the rest of the way. At least he hadn't seen Midnight on his trail since the wolf had run off in the night. Perhaps Midnight had given up. But Coffin knew that he could not let his guard down. Whatever he believed about the wolf, he was well aware of his tracking traits. In the wilderness, the wolf would survive much easier than a man.

Coffin's endurance was breaking down. The effort of carrying Giff for so many miles wore on him. Without proper rest and nourishment he feared that he would not make it to the spike cabins. If he failed they would both die. There was no doubt.

He estimated that they were no more than nine or ten miles from the cabins. Ten miles. Still half the distance to go. Given his present weary condition it now seemed an impossible task. But Coffin resolved that as long as he breathed life he would continue on. Giving up, admitting defeat to the elements, to be destroyed by the environment he cherished? Never, Coffin swore.

He struggled on.

*   *   *

A new storm was coming. The skies were filling with a heavy blanket of deep clouds, swiftly moving over the treetops. It was coming on sundown and Coffin was in the sloping wall of a valley that led to a woodland not a mile away. He had to make it up the slope and into the shelter of the trees where he could build a fire. He would not survive out in the open.

Giff was now fever-ridden and Coffin feared the cough deep in his chest was pneumonia. Their time was running out.

Coffin summoned a reserve of effort and fought his way up the long hill, pushing himself beyond his capabilities. His frosted breath filled the air around his head like a cloud and ice hung from his beard like a frozen crystal mask. His lungs were bursting and pain ran through every portion of his body. His legs were like stone as he defied the drag of gravity and forced one after the other in his driving quest.

By now, he believed the pain in his left foot was definitely frostbite. It was getting impossible to put any weight on that foot. He had once lost a toe to frostbite and it never worried him that much. It was something that he had learned to deal with. But he knew men who had died from it when not treated in time.

Just a little more, he thought. That's all. Maybe ten miles at most. He used to do that much whistling.

Coffin collapsed near the crest of the slope. He passed out.

*   *   *

Coffin awoke to a tugging on his leg and a low roar in his ears. "Coffin," Giff called weakly. "Coffin, listen."

Coffin lifted himself and turned to the distraction. The noise came from somewhere above them. It was a snowmobile coming over the top of a hill directly at the two men.

"Coffin, a snowmobile!" Giff gasped.

"I'll be damned," Coffin said weakly.

*   *   *

Jim Fuller got a phone call from people in New York City two days after Coffin and Giff Taylor took off for Fairbanks. Giff did not show up for his father's funeral and could not be found. When Fuller checked with the airport at Fairbanks he discovered that Coffin had not landed and that his plane was missing. It took a while, and more checking, before Fuller realized that something had happened to the two men.

He arranged for a search party and they set out on snowmobiles. The lost men's trail was tracked to where they were found. The men were only six miles from the spike cabins when they were rescued before the storm broke.

Coffin lost three toes on his left foot and Giff was treated for his broken leg. The cough was pneumonia but was caught in time.

*   *   *

Midnight pushed on through the woods. He was a lone wolf again. The one remaining wolf from the pack was killed by the booming death noise of man. Midnight pushed on alone. His trailing instinct took over as he pursued a single objective, moving relentlessly in one direction, not varying from his set course.

He stopped only to rest and hunt when he was distracted by hunger. In a few weeks he had covered hundreds of miles, urged on by a purposeful determination and guided by an unfailing instinct of the route and its ultimate end. He knew exactly where he was going and there was nothing that stood in his way.

The pain in his right flank had become no more than an annoying throb that he all but ignored. It was caused by the slug from Coffin's .45 that had grazed him and had torn only a piece of flesh away. The man had caused the pain in his leg and had destroyed the pack. He had killed Moon and his two yearlings. The man had inflicted misery on Midnight's existence. He knew the man. He knew him well.

CHAPTER 24

When Miles Coffin finally returned to his house he knew immediately he would not remain here. It was over a month since he had been back and the memory of Lucy was a force he could not reckon with in these surroundings.

His left foot was bandaged and he walked with a crutch. He spent a short while in a hospital, during which time he was charged with the crime of hunting and killing wolves from his plane. He knew this was bound to happen when he deliberately took his chances and broke the law. His plane was wrecked, but might be salvaged, he was told. It would be confiscated by the authorities no matter what he did.

He rented a car with automatic drive since his left leg would not permit him to use a clutch. He found quite a bit of mail waiting for him at the post office; unpaid bills, junk mail, even a letter from Giff Taylor. He waited until he got home before he read it. Giff started by apologizing for the bad start he had made with Coffin, continuing with Andy's having to cope with his recovering left arm, and ended by thanking Coffin for saving him. Giff went on to say that Coffin did not have to worry about lawyers or expense. That problem would be Giff's pleasure; he said he owed him one.

Coffin dropped the mail on a table. It was dusk, the sun just setting. He flipped a light switch and reminded himself that he had neglected the generator. It might be low on fuel and on the verge of running out, he thought. If the temperature dropped below freezing for any length of time there could be other problems with the house.

He ran the water in all the outlets and breathed a sigh of relief. There apparently were no broken pipes. It was chilly in the house, so he got a fire going and poured himself a bourbon while he went through the rest of the mail.

What to do, he wondered. He had to settle with the authorities and might even serve a jail term. That he could bear. What he could not tolerate was the memory of Lucy on those terrible nights that he knew were bound to come. He had few choices. He could sell the place, put it in the hands of a real estate agent and leave. He couldn't conceive anyone wanting to buy a place this far from town. Or he could simply walk away, abandon it and close that door of his life, although he doubted he ever could.

As the sun vanished he threw on his coat and went outside to the shed on the side of the house where the generator and fuel were kept. He fueled the apparatus and kept it going. Lights in the house cast their yellow glow on the melting snow around the house as darkness took over.

As he returned to the front of the house something moved in the pine trees by the fenced compound where the wolves had once lived. The shape was hardly discernible, almost hidden in the dim light, practically lost in its dreary surroundings, but the green eyes that shone in the dark were unmistakable. Coffin knew immediately. It was a wolf.

Fear lodged in Coffin's throat and his pulse pounded.

It must be Midnight. He too had returned home.

Coffin's first thought was to run, but that would not happen. His .45 automatic was inside the house. He knew the wolf could run him down and kill him without his weapon. With his damaged foot he didn't have a prayer of making it into the house before the wolf covered the same distance. It didn't look good for him, he thought, as he began backing up.

His only chance was to cautiously work his way to the doorway, keeping Midnight in front of him, not making any sudden move which might incite the wolf to charge. Midnight survived because of his savagery. Only the strongest survive in the unforgiving wilderness. And, at this precise moment, Coffin realized he was not the stronger. Without the gun, man, the hunter, could not stand up to the wolf, the real hunter. In the predator's environment, unarmed and alone, man was not equal to the animal who survived daily by its ability to kill large game. Coffin had always known this and had always been prepared. Just in case. But now he had become prey for the hunter, the kind of prey on which the wolf survives, the weak, the sickly, ready to die. This time the odds of defeating Coffin were completely in the wolf's favor.

Coffin inched back slowly, keeping his front exposed to the wolf all the time. He began to speak to Midnight, deeply, in a commanding voice that said he was still in charge.

"MIDNIGHT," Coffin shouted, fighting to keep the tremor from his voice lest the wolf would suspect fear. "MIDNIGHT, STAY THERE," he commanded, hoping once again he could bluff the wolf into accepting and obeying his orders.

The wolf growled slowly and stepped out of the gloom.

"STAY, MIDNIGHT," Coffin insisted.

The front door was over fifty feet from him. The wolf was at least that distance away in the opposite direction. Coffin would never make it. As he backed up the wolf came closer. It was not going to work. Not this time. The wolf had made up his mind. He had to stop the beast where he stood.

He needed a weapon. Something. Anything that would deter the wolf momentarily, stall his approach. Coffin glanced around him. To his left was a wood pile, but it was closer to the house than it was to him. There was an ax stuck in the pile of logs, its handle flaunting its presence like a welcoming, beckoning hand. He would never make it. If he could get that far, he might as well try for the front door. At least in the house he could get his gun.

His only hope, he concluded, was to continue his slow retreat and pray the wolf would not charge. But as he backed up Midnight moved towards him step for step.

The wolf was slowly gaining ground, Coffin thought, feeling the sweat on his body, despite the cold evening. He might be able to maintain this distance if he didn't lose his control. Perhaps Midnight was just as frightened as he was. The wolf feared him equally as he did the wolf. Midnight did not know he had no weapon.

Slowly, the distance to the front door lessened. But the wolf was still advancing, his posture threatening. Coffin knew well that Midnight intended to kill him, but up to now he was stalking him as prey, checking him out for battle. The wolf was winning the standoff. The space between them was growing smaller. Midnight was ultimately moving to within striking distance.

In the light from the house Coffin saw him clearly now. The wolf sought his enemy's eyes and locked on them, seeking a sign of weakness. The animal could tell when his opponent was ready to give up his life and he knew when to strike. Coffin tried not to blink until the wolf broke contact.

Coffin felt the confrontation must end in the next few seconds. He burst to his left and made a frantic, stumbling run for the wood pile. He fell across it and both hands grabbed the ax handle, taking it with him over the logs in a crashing collision with the ground.

The wolf was on him in an instant. Midnight cleared the woodpile and came down on Coffin, ready for the kill. Coffin swung the ax and connected. He caught the wolf in the ribs with the blunt end of the ax and drove him off his stride and out of the way. It was enough for Coffin to get to his feet and stumble the short distance to the front door.

The wolf was momentarily stunned, the wind knocked from him.

Coffin made it to the door, the ax still in his hands. He fell through the opening, stumbled and crashed to the floor. He shoved at the door with the ax, trying to close it, but failed to lock it.

The gun. He had to get the gun. Where was it? His coat. On the other side of the room, on the couch. He got to his feet, using the ax as a crutch and scrambled across the floor.

Behind him the door exploded inward as the huge wolf catapulted into the house. Midnight plunged through the barrier, almost knocking the unlatched door from its hinges. The giant animal hit the floor, bounced once on all fours and landed on Coffin's back.

He drove his enemy to the floor on his stomach. The ax was knocked from Coffin's hands as the brute force of the wolf crashed him down.

The massive jaws closed on Coffin's throat and crushed his neck. The teeth, like the spikes of a steel trap, ripped through vital blood vessels.

Coffin knew his death was at hand. Midnight was tearing the life out of him and there was nothing he could do to stop him. He thought of Lucy and how fearful it must have been for her to die like this. He no longer fought the wolf. He gave in to a death at the jaws of a wolf he had taught not to fear him.

Coffin heard his own voice crying out Lucy's name in a pathetic lament as he died.

CHAPTER 25

Maxwell Taylor's death was announced in the newspapers and on television; both readers and viewers were greeted with a similar news item.

"It is a sad commentary," one newsman stated, "that the man who had been so vehement in his fight to continue to use animals as tests for his cosmetics firm spent the last days of his life hunting in Alaska. Reports have it that Mr. Taylor had been in bad health. It is also ironic that Maxwell Taylor was said to have been hunting wolves on what proved to be his last hunt. According to lore, there has never been an unprovoked attack on a human by wolves in North America. Why, then, does man find it necessary to kill these animals? Does the hunter think that wiping out any animal that cannot defend itself is a sport. . . ?"

* * *

Giff came into the board meeting with the same energetic, arrogant spring in his walk, impeccably dressed, as always, and sat in Maxwell Taylor's chair. It was his image that was now mirrored in the polished surface of the conference table. He lit a cigar and exhaled blue smoke in a cloud over his head. He was surrounded by familiar faces he had known for years, the officers of the company. He had been with most of them, alongside them, while Max ran the company. He knew almost every person's policy towards Max. Now he would test their loyalty to the Old Man and to him. He knew that most favored his view towards spinning Taylor Cosmetics public.

"First order of business," he announced, "is that we are taking this company public. Going public will give us the capital to expand in the grand style this company deserves. We are long overdue to bring this company into the future where we belong. We are breaking with old-fashioned ideas that chain us to the past. Antiquated thinking is unacceptable. And . . ." he paused for dramatic effect, "this move will make all of us rich." He paused while murmurs and broad smiles spread around the room.

"Any objections?" he asked. The officers were silent.

"Next," he said "is the 'save the rabbit' fanatics. Anyone have suggestions?"

The executive officers seated around the huge conference table shifted and ruffled papers, glancing at one another for someone to end the silence and offer a breakthrough comment. No one spoke.

"Come on," Giff urged. "Someone must want to say something. We have a public relations problem here that just isn't going away."

Still, no one broke the silence.

"Well, here's my solution to the problem," Giff said firmly. "If it isn't the Draize test with rabbits it will be something else. So I say . . . fuck them all."

There was an instant grumbling around the table. A woman executive finally spoke up, obviously perplexed. "Did I hear you correctly, Mr. Taylor? Did you say. . . ?"

"Fuck 'em!" Giff said again.

He was now in the driver's seat.

* * *

Andy entered Josie Monroe's office at the Exemplar Gallery as soon as he had recovered. She welcomed him with an overlong hug. When she tried to kiss him he backed off. Andy sensed that she became aware of the hostility in his response.

"Before you say anything, Josie," he said, to cut off any excuse she might offer for conspiring with Max Taylor. "I've decided to open my own gallery. You won't be handling my work anymore."

She wasn't sure how to answer. Was his action because of her deal with Max Taylor or was it merely the young man growing up?

"But you have a contract with me," was all she could think to say.

"Really. Then I suggest you sue me."

Later, Andy struggled with a canvas. The therapy he had received for his left arm had so far produced only modest results. He was able to clutch and lift items he used so often in his studio. But he lacked the dexterity in his fingers to manipulate small things. Microsurgery had reattached severed tendons in his shoulder and strenuous exercise had helped rebuild the damaged muscles, but he still had a long way to go to get his arm and hand useful again. He resigned himself to the fact that he would never regain complete use of the limb.

He started sketching the painting with broad strokes. He painted loosely on the prepared white surface, using a thin wash of light blue. It was a basic underpainting for structure and tone, defining shading and composition.

At first glance an observer might only guess at what was taking shape on the canvas but was clearly defined in the artist's mind. Within a few hours the subject of the painting was obvious. It was a large wolf charging out of a background of snow-covered woodland, leaping from the ground as if to vault out of the painting directly at the observer.

Andy had researched photos and drawings of the wolf in libraries and wildlife magazines and had made many sketches until he had decided on the composition for the painting. First came composition. His realistic style, he found, was absolutely suited to wildlife painting. He had discovered a subject that was broad in scope and totally answered his needs. He planned many trips into the wilderness to study the subjects he intended to paint. The money to pursue his new goals came from a trust Max Taylor had set up for him years ago.

In time, the arm would get better and he would be able to paint outdoors. In the meantime he relied a great deal on a camera.

He smiled, thinking of all the years ahead and the work to be done. He imagined himself trekking through the endless wilderness of the great north, photographing and painting what he could never truly understand but at least could attempt to duplicate on canvas. The trip with Max and Giff had served this one purpose, he had found the soul that was missing from his work.

*   *   *

Midnight left the man to die and crossed the open area by the pen where he was raised. He went into the woods, heading north, cutting a straight, deliberate trail away from this place of man.

In the battle with the man, he had suffered bruised ribs when the hard object crashed into his side. The pain slowed him down, but would not deter his journey. He was a lone wolf. He would start over, find a new pack of wolves, somewhere away from man and his death machines. He would mate again and have offspring. He would lead the wolves. They would hunt, grow, play and live together as a social family.

And the cycle would continue.

THE END

AFTERWARD

In order to create a work of fiction involving animals in the wild I have taken certain creative liberties with the wolf to maintain the flow of the story plot. There have been practically no incidents of wolves attacking man in North America, but it is possible that some have happened and not been reported. In this story, the existing laws allowing the hunting of wolves in certain areas of Alaska (as of the late nineteen eighties) are utilized.

Thanks to the Alaska Department of Fish and Game for providing information and maps on game management units and conditions by which wolves may be hunted.

Mike Walsh
Syosset, NY August, 2002

BVG